God, She Hadn't Changed At All.

He had told himself a thousand times since she'd left that she wasn't beautiful. That she wasn't special. That she was just another brown-eyed blonde with long legs, a handful of freckles and a slight overbite.

He had lied. She was back and she was beautiful. She was standing on the sidewalk across the street, the sun dancing off her hair, and she was looking right at him with those gentle doe eyes of hers, sending roughly a thousand volts right down to the soles of his feet.

The driver of the car behind him sat on his horn, and Tucker came back to earth and looked over to find his secretary watching him with an extremely curious look on her face. He let out the clutch too fast and almost stalled.

Cursing quietly, he turned left on Petree Street and crossed the bridge. His secretary hadn't spoken a word. He refused to look at her. If he had to face that smirk of hers, he was going to fire her on the spot.

Dear Reader:

Welcome to Silhouette Desire—sensual, compelling, believable love stories written by and for today's woman. When you open the pages of a Silhouette Desire, you open yourself up to a whole new world— a world of promising passion and endless love.

Each and every Silhouette Desire is a wonderful love story that is both sensuous *and* emotional. You're with the hero and heroine each and every step of the way—from their first meeting, to their first kiss . . . to their happy ending. You'll experience all the deep joys—and occasional tribulations—of falling in love.

In future months, look for Silhouette Desire novels from some of your favorite authors, such as Naomi Horton, Nancy Martin, Linda Lael Miller and Lass Small, just to name a few.

So go wild with Desire. You'll be glad you did!

Lucia Macro
Senior Editor

DIXIE BROWNING

TWICE IN A BLUE MOON

SILHOUETTE *Desire*

Published by Silhouette Books New York

America's Publisher of Contemporary Romance

DIXIE BROWNING

has written over forty books for Silhouette since 1980. She is a charter member of the Romance Writers of America, and *Renegade Player* won a Golden Medallion in 1983. A charismatic lecturer, Dixie has toured extensively for Silhouette Books, participating in "How to Write a Romance" workshops all over the country.

Along with her writing, Dixie has been acclaimed as a watercolor painter, and was the first president of the Watercolor Society of North Carolina. She is currently president of Browning Artworks, Ltd., a gallery featuring fine crafts on Hatteras Island.

One

Tucker Owen left the boardroom, ignored the elevators, and took the stairs. On the ground floor, he strode across the marble lobby, his thoughts still focused on the meeting that had just taken place.

No stranger seeing him for the first time would have taken him for the product of a four-room tar paper shack on the wrong side of the river, despite the fact that his only concession to the occasion was a rather rumpled black tie worn with jeans and a khaki work shirt. He had all the natural assurance of a man who knew exactly where he was headed, a man who stacked up stumbling blocks and turned them into stairways.

Tucker still lived at the same address...and it was still on the wrong side of the river. Yet there was more than a hint of arrogance in his long-limbed stride, although he would have decked the first man who called him that; he considered arrogance purely an attribute of the type of men he had just left.

Yellow. The whole argument, he thought in amazement as he nodded absently to the row of tellers behind the brass-and-glass cages, had been about painting the new community center yellow instead of something deemed more suitable by the damned Ridgebacks gathered in old man Harrington's fourth-floor boardroom.

"I think white would be more, ah—well, a bit more...you know," Brendell had said. Peter Harrington Brendell was fourth generation River Ridge, and he wasn't about to let an upstart from Shacktown forget it. The man drank hot tea in the middle of a steamy June morning and never sweat a drop.

"Well, gray would be all right, you know. I mean, a nice, quiet shade of pale gray is always acceptable over brick." That bit of wisdom had come from bank president George Harrington, Brendell's uncle, who was rumored to have worn gray pin-striped diapers as an infant.

"You want an art gallery? I'll see about getting something lined up once we get the center ticking over. But I warn you right now—you give these kids a white wall, or even pale gray, and you've got yourself an overnight mural."

"Ahhh, graffiti." Old man Harrington touched the point of snowy Irish linen that protruded from his breast pocket, the equivalent of mopping his brow.

Pete Brendell had spoken up to say that yellow could serve as a background for graffiti just as well, but Tucker had stood his ground. His mama had always wanted to paint their house yellow, but they'd never been able to scrape up the money. Besides, brick patterned tar paper didn't take to paint particularly well.

"Well, I'm not sure...." Harrington had grumbled as the meeting had drawn to a close.

"I am," Tucker had said, and his word had carried enough conviction to close the matter. Conviction that came from knowing that not one damned drop of spray paint was going to touch his yellow community center, because every kid east of the river had the word. Tucker had put sweat, blood, and damned near every cent he had into this project. The first would-be Picasso who came near his yellow building with a can of anything thicker than root beer was going to draw back a nub.

"Morning, Gus," he said to a grizzled security guard who, fifteen years before, would have probably collared him on general principle for being anywhere near the bank.

"How do, Tucker. Reckon Donnie's going to bring 'er on home come Sat'day?"

"Just might do it, Gus. He's got the machine, but if I were you, I'd keep my eye on Buck. He's ready to go the distance, and I think this just might be his race."

Tucker fanned the heavy brass door and stepped out into the steam heat of another mid-June morning. Behind him, a row of tellers, momentarily idle, looked through the glass portion of the door at the silhouette of a long, rangy body that veed down from an enviable set of shoulders to a narrow waist and a pair of long, muscular legs that began with a tight clench of hard muscle and ended in a pair of well-worn moccasins.

Unknown to Tucker, there were several ragged sighs. The teller on the far end, a blonde with a brand new backyard tan, said softly, "Boy, he thinks he's God's gift to women, doesn't he?"

"He is," said another one.

"I'd like to be the one to rip off the gift wrappings," said a third, resting her elbows on the cool marble counter.

"Honey, you and me both," a fourth said, sighing.

"Forget it," said the lead teller. "Tucker Owen hasn't dated a single woman more than three times in a row ever since whatsername ran off—that preacher's girl that married Phillips Enterprises, you remember?"

"Hope, wasn't that her name? Whatever happened to the Phillipses, anyway?"

"How about married women?" quipped the blonde.

"Oh-oh, here comes Mr. H.," whispered the lead teller. "Y'all hush up and try to look busy for a change, hear?"

Meanwhile, Tucker, oblivious to the speculation that had followed him out the door, stood for a moment with his hand on the hot metal cab of the blue-and-silver pickup truck bearing the logo, Owen Automotive. He'd told Evelyn he'd be back at the office before noon, and knowing his secretary, she'd have a bunch of letters for his signature, a bunch more phone messages, and after that she'd start hassling him about things he was in no mood to be hassled about.

Such as when he was going to settle down with a nice woman.

When he was damned good and ready, he had told her a thousand times—which would be never.

And if it wasn't that, it would be the Shacktown Community Center. Dammit, it wasn't enough he'd had to take on every taxpayer in Princetown; he'd even had to convince his own secretary that Shacktown was affecting Princetown's economic growth, whether or not they wanted to believe it. Tobacco was hurting—textiles were hurting—a big home-owned trucking firm had just turned belly-up.

Every new business interested in locating in the area looked first at the statistics, and whether or not the business community wanted to believe it, Shacktown was an integral part of Princetown's statistics—crime rate, dropout rate, average income level and all.

The town, named for John Pritz, a ferryman who had carried passengers across the Tar River roughly two hundred years ago, had grown up around both landings. The name had evolved to Princetown about the time the textile and tobacco barons had begun building their mansions up on the high ridge that ran parallel to the winding river, with the working classes settling in the mosquito-ridden lowlands on the other side.

River Ridge had consistently ignored Shacktown and Shacktown had actively resented River Ridge for as long as anyone could recall. Tucker was fed up with the whole situation. They were all one town, he reminded the city fathers. It was time they did something about the living conditions east of the river.

They'd said it would take federal help, and that would take years.

Tucker had said bull—the slumlords weren't in Washington, they were right up there on River Ridge, sipping their gin and tonics and lying about their golf scores.

They'd said, why not something simple, like a pretty little park along that overgrown section of the riverbank.

Tucker had had his own reasons for not wanting to involve that particular section of riverbank. He'd suggested instead, a community center, intending to use it as a wedge to get them involved in his neighborhood.

They'd said it was far too ambitious a project. Couldn't be done. Hell, a few of them had come right out and said it *shouldn't* be done! That it was a waste of good money—it would need ongoing support, and the taxpayers would never stand for it.

Tucker had reminded them that they would be upgrading the property values and thus increasing their tax base. That had caught their attention. He'd finally got them to agree to forming a committee to study the feasibility of doing something about the shameful conditions east of the river.

Meanwhile, Tucker had his own opinion of feasibility studies. While they'd been spending eleven months discussing the feasibility of looking into the situation, he had scraped up enough to buy an old abandoned plug tobacco factory that was rapidly turning into an insurance liability for the owner. Next, he had bullied Shacktown's unemployed and unemployable into hustling their collective butts to get it in shape to scrape by the building inspection.

Once that hurdle had been passed, the rest had been downhill. He'd been able to call in a few favors from some of the big names in stock-car racing, and that had finally brought Princetown's cadre of reluctant philanthropists around.

While the citizens of Shacktown had sweated over the actual labor of dismantling and hauling off outmoded machinery, retarring roofs, sanding and finishing floors, building new partitions and tearing out old ones, and painting the whole thing in colors that defied desecration, Princetown's elite had donned their designer workout togs and blocked traffic for several hours in the name of sweet charity. They had rallied all civic and social organizations around their latest pet project—Shacktown.

And Tucker, elated, had wished a thousand times that his mother were alive to see it all. He wished he had somehow managed to paint their house yellow before she died.

He wished like hell that he had told her he loved her. He could only hope that she had known. Words didn't always come easy to him. Especially words about...that kind of thing.

Two half-grown boys skimmed past him on skateboards, kicking up a hot wind in their wake—reminding him that he'd been standing outside the bank for nearly five minutes—five minutes he couldn't really afford to waste.

Absently, he followed the boys' snaky progress down the sidewalk, wondering why the devil Billy Coe was out fooling around when just last week Tucker had lined him up with a part-time summer job.

Summertime! It was hot and sultry, and it hadn't rained in six weeks. Hell, he couldn't blame Billy for skipping out. He felt like skipping out himself.

Sliding into the ovenlike cab of his truck, he reached for the phone. "Evelyn? Look, something's come up—can you do without me for an hour?"

"If you're planning on eating Lin Tuan's chili for lunch, I'd watch out for rabies if I were you. Been a lot of dogs turned up missing in that neighborhood lately."

"No problem, cooking kills the germs."

"You want me to go ahead and order those valves?"

"Yeah—just duplicate that last order, will you? And tell 'em to ship it air freight."

"You can't afford air freight anymore. You bought a worn out old plug tobacco factory, remember?"

"Hell, ship it by reindeer then—just get it here by day after tomorrow. Oh, and Evelyn—put away your peanuts, fasten your belt and put your shoes back on."

She chuckled over the phone. "You bastard," she said, and hung up.

Tucker headed for the river. He could do without lunch. After being cooped up all morning with a roomful of well-heeled civic leaders, he needed a little fresh air. At least it would be cooler down there. Not much wind could get through the kudzu-covered forest, but green was a helluva lot more soothing than concrete, asphalt and marble.

It was inevitable that he would think of Hope, of course. He hadn't been down to their special place more than a dozen times in the seven years since she'd left, but it hit him every time. Maybe he was one of those guys who got a kick out of pain—or maybe he just needed to remind himself every so often that while he might be able to take on River Ridge's shrewdest business heads, he had been no match for a big-eyed, skinny kid with seven freckles on the south side of her nose and a smile that had melted every bone in his body.

Hope Elizabeth Outlaw. Hope Phillips now. After all these years, he should have forgotten her name, much less what she looked like—that soft, golden glow that seemed to shine around her like a halo.

Some halo! The woman had taken everything he had to give her—or would've given her, if she'd just waited a little while longer—and thrown it back in his face. She'd gone for the gold, and Tucker had taken it in the gut and gone on about his business—gone on functioning, just as if a part of him hadn't withered up and died.

Without leaving his truck, he stared at the river for some twenty minutes or so, trying a little too hard not to remember. And then he got the hell out of there.

* * *

"My car or yours?" Evelyn Hampton asked as Tucker passed by her desk on the way to his own office.

"Huh?" He swung around at the door and stared at the woman who had been his secretary ever since he had taken over Ziglar Motors, where he'd worked as a kid, and turned it into Owen Automotive. He knew for a fact that she was thirty-eight, seven years older than he was. She didn't look a day over thirty, in spite of having two grown kids. Tucker found her indispensable at work, and the only reason he fired her with boring regularity was her tendency to lay her smart mouth on his personal life. Which he damned well didn't need.

"Mayor Bondurant at one-fifteen, remember?"

"Oh, hell, why didn't you remind me?"

"I just did."

"How'd you know I'd be back in time?"

She gave him a look that made him wonder uncomfortably if she didn't know precisely where he'd been, and what he'd been thinking about. "I'm not riding in one of those trucks. I can't climb up that high without splitting my skirt seams. If your car's still on the rack, we'll take mine and I can drop you back here afterward. I'm taking the rest of the afternoon off."

"Are you asking me or telling me?"

"Telling you. Put on your tie and jacket—Ed Bondurant's no stickler, but you can at least make the effort to conform."

"Dammit, I had a tie on all morning! It's the middle of summer. Doesn't anyone around here have a grain of common sense?"

Ten minutes later, Tucker, a rumpled tan jacket slung over his shoulder, held open the driver's side door of Evelyn's convertible. The wearing of ties and coats in the middle of June was a crime against nature. Any man with half a brain knew that.

He glared malevolently at his secretary's cool sleeveless dress. She looked as fresh as a tall glass of iced tea. Women who didn't sweat on the hottest day of summer were a royal pain.

"Why the hell couldn't Bondurant have sat in on this morning's meeting?" he grumbled.

"You drive," Evelyn said, ignoring his foul humor. "I'm not in the mood for your snide remarks about women drivers."

"Quit riding the clutch and swinging two lanes wide on your turns, and you won't hear any. What'd you learn on, anyway—a semi?"

"A 255 Massey-Ferguson," she said, slipping gingerly onto the hot plastic seat. "And the day you can beat me in a tractor pull is the day you can tell me how to drive, macho man." They'd had the same conversation so many times, the words followed automatically.

Tucker slipped behind the wheel of the convertible. He despised the thing, partly because he considered convertibles impractical and ostentatious—especially hot pink ones—but mostly because she had never let him lift her hood, and he was convinced that no engine could function efficiently until it had undergone the magic Tucker Owen overhaul.

The meeting went well, considering he hated meetings. Harrington was in attendance, looking perfectly comfortable in his three-piece suit. Checking to be certain enough studies were done before a penny of the bank's money was spent, Tucker thought sourly.

The mayor got the ball rolling. "Coach from the high school has agreed to work with the kids two afternoons a week, and he'll speak to the assistant coach next week."

A secretary just outside the walnut-paneled office typed noisily. While Evelyn quietly took notes, Mayor Bondurant went on at length about which social services could be expected to participate, and whether or not funds would be forthcoming to hire a full-time maintenance man. The air conditioner droned in the background, and outside the window, two squirrels played hide-and-seek in a pecan tree. Tucker shifted restlessly and wished he were back down by the river.

"I'm pleased to be able to announce that we've found a woman to take on the day-care center," announced George Harrington, and Tucker wondered why the hell he couldn't have said so this morning, instead of insisting they meet in the mayor's office two hours later.

He grunted acknowledgment while Mayor Bondurant rubbed his pudgy freckled hands and said, "Good, good, has Miss Eula decided to come out of retirement?" Miss Eula Finley was an institution around Princetown, having cracked several generations of knuckles in her Kiddy Cat Care Center at the lower end of the River Ridge Road. Hope had worked there on weekends and summers, Tucker remembered with a further hardening of his stern features.

"Naturally, I broached the matter with Miss Eula first, but she suggested I speak to Gabriella Boger. I believe Miss Boger managed the Steak House until it burned down back in February. Of course, I don't know her personally, you understand—"

Tucker understood. Gabby Boger was not exactly Shacktown, but she was definitely not River Ridge, either. Her folks owned a small tobacco farm just north of town.

"Miss Boger's expertise lies in the area of management, but she claims to have someone in mind with experience in the field of child care, and since we're budgeted for two full-time workers and possibly a part-time helper, at least for the first year, I recommend we consider her application."

Tucker's mind, unusually distracted of late, had picked up the name and run with it. Gabby Boger. It set in motion a distinctly unwelcome chain of memories, and he'd never even known the woman all that well. Or rather the girl. She'd been a school friend of Hope's all those years ago, and he'd liked her for that. Hope had needed friends. Tucker had known it even then, although he'd been a little jealous of the few she had, because they were from her own world.

Shifting restlessly in the walnut-and-black leather chair, he tried to shake the strange mood that had assailed him lately. As if he didn't have enough on his mind, it seemed as if everywhere he turned there was something to remind him of what he'd spent the past seven years trying to forget.

"—Miss Boger's résumé—excellent references, and—"

Tucker tuned in and out of the talk around him. God, what an unlikely pair they'd been—dark, gutsy little Gabby pitching herself square into the middle of whatever was going on, and Hope—his little Hope, standing on the sidelines, blushing if anyone noticed her, saying "yes, ma'am" and "no, sir" in that whispery little voice. Shy and overdressed, she'd been a natural target for all the toughest guys in school.

Fortunately, he had been the toughest of the lot. To the young Tucker, Hope had been his princess, he her dragonslayer. Slowly, they had become friends. Slowly, because he hadn't dared to rush things. She had been unlike anyone he had ever met—had ever imagined, and he'd been half afraid of her. But gradually she had come to trust him. She had crept out of her shell, laughing and chattering like a little squirrel. He had been utterly enchanted, and for a while—for years—he had almost forgotten that they came from completely different worlds.

In the beginning, she'd been only a child, and he'd been a man—at least he had considered himself a man at fourteen. For the first several years, he had kept an eye on her from a distance, but after awhile, he'd taken to walking her home from school, always stopping just short of the three-story, turreted parsonage on River Ridge Road.

Then one day he had found her crying. She'd been furious because her parents wouldn't let her try out for the cheerleading team. It was the first time he'd had cause to suspect that there might be more grit and gumption under that pink-and-gold exterior than he'd given her credit for.

She'd told him she wasn't going home until she was good and ready, and to keep her from hanging around the school grounds, where she might get in trouble, he had taken her out to the river on the back of his bike and shown her his special place, where great swags of honeysuckle and kudzu vines made cool green caves of privacy, lapped by the warm, dark waters of the Tar River.

The meeting began to break up around him, and Tucker came back to the present, wondering belatedly if he'd missed anything important. But before he'd even left the building, his thoughts were once more adrift.

She'd been his Hope. And he'd lost her.

"Hey, bossman—you fall asleep in there?" Evelyn taunted as they made their way across the heat-softened pavement. She slid into the passenger's seat, winced, and shoved her hands underneath her thighs.

"I was thinking, that's all." Tucker challenged her with a steely look from blue-gray eyes that were all the more effective for being set off by ebony hair and sun-bronzed skin. "Any law against that?"

"Mighty defensive, aren't we? Want to come to supper tonight? I boiled a ham last night, and there's fresh peas and new potatoes—more than enough for Joe and me."

"Thanks, but I'll just grab a bowl of chili at Lin Tuan's."

"I keep trying to tell you, that stuff'll kill you."

But Tucker's mind had skipped out again. They were passing the Downtown Motel, and he stopped for the light. Glancing around absently, he saw the woman and stiffened instinctively. It wasn't Hope, of course—it never was. He'd been fooled by more than one leggy, vulnerable-looking blonde—you'd think after all this time he would've learned better, but something about this one...

She'd been standing in the door of the motel, and then she stepped out on the sidewalk, into the blinding light of the late afternoon, and Tucker felt as if a hard fist had punched him below the belt.

"Jesus," he breathed.

She was staring back at him, her mouth slightly open. Two boys zoomed past him on skateboards, and Tucker recognized Billy Coe again. Dammit, they were heading right for her!

He yelled a warning the instant before Billy veered past, striking her elbow and knocking her purse to the sidewalk. With a terse oath, Tucker grabbed the door handle just as the light changed and the driver behind sounded on his horn. But even before he could react, Billy had tilted the board around, scooped up her purse, which had fallen several feet away on the sidewalk, and returned it to her.

A car passed by and nearly clipped the door Tucker had started to open. He continued to stare, his mind not on the boy who'd gone sailing off down the sidewalk, but on the woman who still stood there staring at him.

He tried to tell himself he was imagining things. Just because he'd ended up at the river today—just because Gabby Boger's name had come up in the meeting....

God, she hadn't changed at all. He had told himself a thousand times since she'd left that she wasn't beautiful. That she wasn't special. That she was just another brown-eyed blonde with long legs, a handful of freckles and a slight overbite.

He had lied. She was back, and she was beautiful. The sun was dancing off her hair, which she'd braided down the back of her head. Heat had pulled loose tendrils that curled around her face and down on her neck, and she was looking right at him with those gentle doe eyes of hers, sending roughly a thousand volts right down to the soles of his feet.

The driver of the car behind him sat on his horn, and Tucker came back to earth to find Evelyn watching him with an extremely curious look on her face. He let out the clutch too fast and almost stalled.

Cursing quietly, he turned left on Petree, crossed the bridge, then took Pokeberry on out to the shop on Justice Road. Evelyn hadn't spoken a word. He refused to look at her. If he had to face that smirk of hers, he was going to fire her on the spot!

And this time she just might take him seriously.

By the time Gabby pulled up to the curb, Hope had her breathing back under control. Her knees had decided to support her and her heart had resumed a more or less normal rhythm. Hurrying around to the passenger side, she slid in. "Gabby, I'm afraid this isn't a very good idea."

"What, eating? Believe me, it's a great idea. After awhile, it even gets to be a habit, honest."

"No, silly—I meant my coming back to Princetown." When she'd agreed on the spur of the moment to come back and go into business with her old friend, Hope's spirits had been at their lowest ebb. Even so, she had thought it over carefully—what it would mean going back to the town she had left so hurriedly seven years before.

If she'd thought about Tucker—and of course she had, almost every day of those seven endless years—she had fully believed he would have long since left Princetown. What was there to keep him? His parents were both dead. He would have earned his engineering degree long before now, even working his way through school. She'd thought he might have stayed on in Atlanta.

"Well, I don't know about you, but I'm starving. Sorry I had to dump you off at the motel right at lunchtime, but there was this tooth—God, I'm still numb. Remind me not to order hot coffee, will you?"

"That's all right, I had a snack on the plane. I'm not all that hungry."

"You can eat a barbecue though, right?"

Hope smiled in agreement, her mind not on barbecue but on the man she had just seen after what seemed a lifetime.

Dear Lord, he hadn't changed a bit!

Yes, he had, too. Oh, not physically—at least, not that she'd been able to see in that one quick glimpse. But he looked so hard. In fact, he'd looked at her almost as if he *hated* her.

But that was crazy. Why would Tucker have hated her? If anything, she should be the one to hate him. Hadn't he done everything in his power to make her love him—which hadn't been all that hard to do—while he'd never had the slightest intention of loving her back?

At first she'd thought it was just that terrible pride of his, because he was from Shacktown and she was from River Ridge. She'd tried to make him understand that the parsonage had nothing to do with her personally—the one they'd lived in before coming to River Ridge Baptist had been a two bedroom, one bathroom bungalow with mice and mildew, and a gutter that had dumped all over the front steps every time it rained.

Pride. Hope had never quite known how much of Tucker's reticence was stiff-necked pride and how much was simply a lack of caring. He'd coddled her and protected her as a child, and later on, when she'd been old enough to want more, he had taught her all she knew—which was still damned little—about love.

It hadn't been enough for her, and evidently, *she* hadn't been enough for him. He could certainly have had her if he'd been interested. She had practically begged him to take her that last summer when he'd stolen a week from the demanding co-op plan that was putting him through engineering school.

"So what's not a good idea, then?"

"What?"

"You said something wasn't a good idea," Gabby reminded her.

Hope wrenched her mind back to the present. "I told you—my coming back. The day-care thing. Maybe I should have stayed in Boston and looked for another job. They can't all pay slave wages—I saw some pretty well-fed people up there."

"Forget Boston, you're back home now. I remember a time when you'd have given your eye teeth for a chance like this. Like I told you when I called, they're giving us a free hand in setting it up and running it. It'll be ours, Hope—*ours*! And once we've got our act down pat, why then, we get a loan and open another one, and then another. Boger-Phillips, Limited, how does that sound? Or maybe Hope and Gabby, Inc...."

Hope had to laugh. "You're nuts, you know that? Who in their right mind would want to franchise day-care centers?"

"Listen, that's where the money is. How many women these days are staying home to look after their own kids?"

"How many rich day-care operators do you know?" Hope countered. She was amused at her friend's aggressive tendencies. It was nothing new—Gabby had been talking about how to double the restaurant's business even while she'd been flipping burgers at the Hamburger Hut back in their high school days.

"Miss Eula made a living at it for a hundred years."

"Miss Eula made a living at it because she was the only one in town with the guts and the energy to take on the job, but things are different now. There are all sorts of regulations, and I don't know diddly about that end of the business. That was Miss Eula's province—mine was cookies, juice, bandages and Simon Says. Gabby, we could get into trouble over our heads before we even realized it."

"No way. When it comes to rules, regs, and handling bureaucrats, we've got it made in the shade. You think the B.O.H. boys didn't examine everything from the soles of my shoes to the insides of my rubber gloves when I was managing the Steak House? You think the guys at the franchise places back when I was running the Hamburger Hut weren't just dying to see me slip down a grade? Ha! This is going to be the best run day-care center in the state of North Carolina. I mean, they're only kids, aren't they? We keep 'em from killing each other for a few hours, wipe a few noses, hand out the cookies and juice, and bingo!''

"Bingo, nothing. I can see right now, you're going to be a lot of help."

They discussed the matter in detail, with Gabby growing more and more enthusiastic and Hope more and more reluctant. Not because she wasn't interested, but because Tucker was back home. And for all she knew, he had a wife and children of his own.

What if he brought his children for her to look after? It would kill her! He wouldn't, not if he had an ounce of sensitivity.

Still, it was a possibility she was going to have to face. The center was for the residents of Shacktown, and Tucker had once been a resident—might still be for all she knew, although it was hardly likely. That fuchsia convertible hadn't looked like Shacktown, and neither had the lush auburn-haired woman in the blue dress.

"Honey, it's a little late for second thoughts. I've already sworn a blood oath to take on the neighborhood creepers and crawlers, and despite the fact that I helped raise six younger brothers and sisters, we both know I can't handle it alone. You're the one with all the patience. I'd probably stuff their little yappers full of candy the first time they let out a squawk."

Hope had to smile. "Well, for starters, you can stop making our clients sound like a swarm of insects. Whatever happened to that restaurant you were planning on owning by the time you were thirty?"

Gabby pulled into the parking of the barbecue house and shut off the engine. "I've still got a couple of years. Anyhow, restaurants are a dime a dozen—the competition'll give you ulcers even if the food doesn't, but kid-keepers . . . now there's a necessity. I hear it all the time—whenever two women get together, you know what they talk about? Baby-sitters. Dependable people to look after their kids while they go off and fulfill themselves or bring home the Baco-Bits or whatever.''

Gabby slung her sun-browned legs out of the car and collected her purse. ''All it takes to be a success is find out what the public wants and give it to 'em. We'll start out working our tails off for peanuts, and first thing you know, we'll be ready to make our move.''

Frowning, Hope followed her into the air-conditioned restaurant. ''Why do I feel like boarding the next plane for Boston and begging Henrietta's to give me my old job back?''

Gabby signaled for two chopped barbecues and two iced teas and turned to her friend. ''Look, honey, I did this for your own good. Pushing perfume at a fancy boutique won't support you once the insurance runs out, and you know it.''

''It ran out last month, and my rent jumped thirty dollars a month back in January, and you're right—I couldn't have baited a mouse trap with what was left after all the deductions, but all the same...''

''If you're worried about seeing Tucker Owen again, don't.''

Hope's already pale face went two shades paler, making her freckles stand out like a spattering of paint. ''I don't— How did you—?''

''Oh, honey, do you think I didn't know how things were with you two that last summer? The whole town knew! Why do you think your parents were so damned anxious to get you safely married to Hugh, even after the Phillipses moved away?''

Tucker could have finished his car up in half an hour and driven home. He left her on the rack and walked. It was only seven blocks to the house on the corner of Pine and Bias Streets—the house that had once been little more than a tar paper shack, but which now boasted a new roof, a new front porch and several thousand dollars' worth of new plumbing. Not to mention a fresh coat of yellow paint, and a set of moss-green shutters.

Once home, he got a beer and took it outside, passing up the new porch furniture in favor of the concrete steps. They were cool, at least. Maybe he needed the feel of something cold and hard under his rear end to take his mind off the way he'd been feeling ever since he'd seen her standing there outside the Downtown Motel.

Hope Outlaw. Tall, sun-streaked blonde, big doe eyes the color of melted chocolate… And she was built like a model, from her cheekbones right down to the high arches of her narrow feet. The only thing lacking was the self-confidence. She'd never been permitted to develop that.

At least she hadn't back when he'd known her, before she'd run off and married that damn Ridgeback, Hugh Phillips.

To think he'd once considered her the princess of his own private kingdom. That was a laugh! In those days, his private kingdom had been a leaky four-room shack that smelled of gin and collard greens. He wouldn't have let her come within a country mile of his so-called kingdom.

Hope. Even her name had gotten to him. There'd been this sort of shining quality about her, right from the very first time he'd ever laid eyes on her. It was like she had a light on inside her that shone right through her skin and all, and he'd been half-afraid to touch her for fear he might short out whatever it was that made her glow that way.

It was only because the rest of his life had been so gray and hopeless, Tucker had told himself a hundred times. A thousand times. Especially after she'd left.

Reluctantly, he gave in to the memories. He could still remember everything about that first day. The heat. The brassy look of the sky. The smell of dust and fried onions, honeysuckle and motor oil. Her old man had been the new preacher at River Ridge Baptist, and there'd been this big old moving van and a new Buick station wagon parked outside the parsonage.

Tucker had driven his old man's pickup over to the Handy Pantry for hot dogs, because there'd been nothing in the house to eat, as usual. He'd seen the moving van turn off the interstate and he'd followed it into town, partly out of curiosity, but mostly because he was driving without a license and he happened to know that both smokies were over at Lin Tuan's Diner eating lunch.

It had been his way of flipping off the whole damned town. He'd been fourteen at the time, and tough the way only an overgrown kid with an overgrown chip on his shoulder can be tough. At fourteen he'd already been pushing six feet, and ready to take on the world bare-fisted.

Hope had been nine. Yellow-haired, skinny legged and squeaky clean. Tucker thought he'd never seen anything so clean in all his born days. He'd sort of hated her on sight, but in those days, he'd hated just about everything. Especially everything west of the Tar River.

He'd known even back then that he would have to get away before the town killed him. What had made him clench up so bad he could hardy talk had been the fact that he couldn't see how he was going to do it. Not with Ma the way she was and Pa drinking up the few bucks he managed to earn pushing broom down at Proctor's Hardware. Four, five times a week, the old man would come home knee-walking drunk, bellowing out, "I gotta light an' I'm gonna let it shine," and if they didn't sing along with him, he'd start cussing Ma and then he'd light into Tucker.

Which was a damned sight better than the other way around, because Tucker could handle him. Tucker could handle just about anything in those days.

Fourteen. God, he'd been tough then. He'd as soon knock a guy down as step out of his way—especially if the dude happened to be wearing white chinos and one of those shirts with the flip-tailed alligator, which was what all the River Ridge kids had been wearing that summer.

He'd hung out at the school looking tough and waiting for a chance to glare at Hope. She'd been scared to death of him the first few times, but pretty soon, she'd just stared back at him, her big eyes looking like she didn't know whether to run or to belt him one.

The first time she'd smiled at him, he'd said something so filthy she hadn't even recognized it, and feeling like raw sewage, he'd gone off and picked a fight with a two-hundred-pound jock on the football team.

He'd been sixteen the first time he'd ever met her father. If memory served him, his first words had been, "Preacher Outlaw. Ha! Good joke!"

He'd been arranging his mother's funeral, hurting some kind of bad and scared stiff someone would notice and feel sorry for him. Pa had drunk himself unconscious the night she'd died, so the whole matter had fallen to Tucker. He'd been determined to send her off from River Ridge Baptist, because once, a long time ago, before she'd got into trouble and had to marry Pa, she'd been a member there.

He hadn't known if her name was still on the roll—he hadn't asked. If Dr. Outlaw had refused to perform the service, Tucker would probably have taken the place apart barehanded, but to his credit, the man had treated him just like anyone else in need.

Hope had been there. At the service. She and her mother had sung in the choir—something slow and dreary. He'd hated her then because she'd looked so clean and pretty she'd made him want to cry. She'd been eleven then, already tall for her age. Already beautiful in a long-legged, big-eyed way that had grabbed hold of him and just about wrung him dry.

Sighing, Tucker finished off his beer and got stiffly to his feet. He felt old tonight. Older than usual. Maybe it was seeing Hope again. Maybe it was just rehashing ancient history. She hadn't really changed all that much—evidently, marriage had agreed with her. But he'd aged a hundred years or so.

Hell, he'd been a hundred years old when he was sixteen—so what did that make him now?

Answering his own unspoken question, Tucker went inside and picked up the phone, dialing a number he hadn't
called in several months. He preferred to think it was because he'd been too tied up in the red tape of getting the
center launched, but self-honesty forced him to confess that
it had been more a lack of interest.

"Josie? It's Tuck Owen. Got anything on for tonight?"

A few minutes later he replaced the phone, feeling somewhat better. If there was a slightly more defensive look
about him than usual, Tucker would be the last one to recognize it. Maybe he'd been born on the defensive. Old habits die hard.

Tonight, he told himself, he needed to unwind. Come tomorrow, he was going to have to get in touch with Gabby
Boger and find out just what kind of a setup she was going
to need, and who she had lined up to work with her. It was
a long shot—the rest of the committee might not go for it,
but he'd kind of like to work Billy's mother, Wanda Coe, in
there somewhere if he could swing it. He knew damned well
she needed the money. Wanda had been good to his mother
when she was sick, and Tucker owed her a lot for that. Besides, part of Billy's problem was the way his mother was
going about earning their keep.

But the problems of a woman trying to raise a half-grown
kid alone weren't all that was on his mind as he shucked off
his jeans and stroked the late-day stubble on his jaw.

Gabby and Hope had been close friends a long time ago.
For all he knew, they could've kept in touch. And Hope had
worked part time for old Miss Eula while all the other kids
had worked at fast-food places. It had bugged the hell out
of her that her parents wouldn't let her work where all the
kids hung out, but she'd sort of liked it—working with
children. She'd been good at it, too, because he'd come by
one morning while she had 'em all lined up out under Miss
Eula's big old oak tree, telling them some wild story about
pirates and kings and princes and princesses....

He'd listened, not admitting even to himself that he'd got a kick out of the story. Yeah, she'd been good at it—she'd had 'em all under her spell, even him. Especially him, he thought wryly.

But then, what the devil would a rich and beautiful young widow be doing working for peanuts in a community center day-care facility? In Shacktown, yet!

Civic duty? Social conscience?

Hell no! It was just a coincidence that she'd happened to turn up about the same time they'd been looking for someone to take on the job, he told himself as he stepped out of the shower in his new yellow-and-white bathroom. No reason why a woman couldn't come back to visit her old home. No reason at all, he reassured himself—just as long as she got out of town before she caused any trouble.

Two

Once again Hope was waiting outside the motel when Gabby pulled up at the curb. Three convertibles had passed by since she had stepped outside. None of them had been hot pink, yet she was unconsciously braced, remembering every tiny detail of the way Tucker had looked the day before. His hair, still that deep shade of brown that was nearly black, had been ruffled by the wind. Her hands curled now as if they could actually feel the soft, vital texture.

He'd been wearing a short-sleeved khaki shirt unbuttoned halfway down his chest, a dark tie draped casually around his neck, but not tied. She'd seen him the instant before he had spotted her, and even in her stunned condition, there had been no mistaking that look of bitter disbelief that had crossed his face a moment before his features had gone hard and still.

The woman beside him had looked vaguely familiar, but Hope couldn't place her. Hardly surprising, considering that her social circle had been so limited, due partly to her par-

ents' strictness and partly to the shyness that had afflicted
her back then.

Where were they going? Where had they been? What were
they doing together at that hour of the day? Those questions and a hundred more had flashed through her mind in
the few seconds they'd stared at one another.

Was Tucker seriously involved with her? She was certainly beautiful enough—in a ripe sort of way. They hadn't
seemed all that wrapped up in each other. In fact, they'd
seemed to be ignoring each other, the way people did when
they'd been married long enough for the newness to wear
off.

"I could have walked to this meeting," she said now,
fastening her seat belt. "The bank's not that far."

"We're not meeting at the bank, didn't I tell you?"

"I'm beginning to think there are several things you
haven't told me." Hope bit her lip. What on earth was she
doing back in North Carolina again, on the basis of a few
brief, excited phone calls? They hadn't seen each other in
seven years! People could do a lot of changing in that length
of time. Lord knows, she had.

Still, Gabby had once been her closest friend, which
counted for something. Counted for a lot, actually. The
trouble was, they'd drifted apart, swapping birthday and
Christmas cards with chatty, meaningless messages scrib-
bled around the verse, as if that could make up for time and
distance apart.

All Hope knew about the woman beside her was that she
still hadn't accomplished her lifelong dream of owning her
own business by the time she was thirty.

All Gabby could know about Hope was that she had
hurriedly run off and married the boy next door, and been
left a widow four years later. That was all Hope wanted
anyone to know. Her own lack of backbone had gotten her
into the sham marriage in the first place. Hugh's death had
left her with little but battered pride and a big stack of bills,
which she had spent the next three years paying off.

Gabby's phone call had come at a time when Hope had been at her lowest ebb. Her own parents were in Scotland taking part in an international exchange program sponsored by her father's church. Hugh's mother had died two years after Hugh had been injured, and within six months, Bob Ed had remarried and moved away from Boston. Hope had been facing an increase in her rent and a dead end in her career—if selling cosmetics at a neighborhood boutique and typing term papers at home could be called a career.

"Sorry I talked you into coming back home?" asked Gabby. Her instincts had always been sharp as a squirrel's tooth.

"I'm just beginning to realize what we've got ourselves into. You say that contract's legally binding even without my signature?"

"Probably not, but you wouldn't back out on me now, would you? I've already signed away a year of my life, and we both know I can't handle it by myself. The business end, sure, but all those kids? Uh-uh!"

"The pay isn't even as much as I earned in Boston," Hope said, her feet growing colder by the moment. "I must have been off my rocker to let you talk me into this thing."

"Come on—It took all of three minutes to talk you into throwing in with me, and anyway, the cost of living down here is a heck of a lot better than it is in Boston. We'll start out breaking even, with nowhere to go but up. And I already told you we can move another bed into my apartment. I'm checking on it right now."

"Okay, but this committee of yours . . ."

"Not mine. They're just a bunch of old fuddies who handle the funding for the center, that's all."

"*Which* old fuddies?" Hope had a funny feeling she wasn't going to like the answer. With absolutely nothing to go on, she was beginning to grow suspicious. It wasn't like Gabby to be evasive, but not once had she mentioned a single thing about who they'd be answering to.

"Oh, by the way, did I tell you I heard Elsie Brendell—that's Pete Brendell's wife—he's one of them. And his uncle George Harrington, who's president of the bank. Anyhow, Elsie went to this place up in Virginia and got herself a facelift, and they say when she came home, Pete pitched a deep-fried fit, claiming she looked like a nubile Chinaman. No kidding, she hasn't got a single wrinkle, and I happen to know she was born the same year as my daddy, and he was born in nineteen and thirty!"

Hope repressed a smile. From habit, she searched for something nice to say about the woman in question, as if it could take away the sting of criticism. "The Brendells were always friendly to Mama and Daddy when we lived here. They used to invite me to swim in their pool and there was always a maid standing by with a long chrome pole. I used to be scared to death—I thought she was going to hit me with it if I didn't behave."

"Oh, Lawsy, Hope, you were such an idiot. But a sweet one."

"I don't know about sweet, but I was definitely an idiot. I'm working on it, though. Gabby, are you sure it's all right—my moving in with you, I mean? I can afford to take a room somewhere."

"No way! You're coming in with me, and we're going to have a ball, I promise you!"

Hope wasn't interested in having a ball. She wouldn't have known how to go about it if she were. All she wanted now was to bring a measure of stability to her own life, and she had thought that living among people who had known her parents—who had watched her grow up—might do that.

Now she wasn't quite so sure.

"Whoops!" The dark-haired woman in the white cotton dress, plastic watermelons dangling from her ears, grinned and pressed one red espadrilled foot to the floor as they approached a stretch of rough pavement. Gabby looked on potholes as a personal challenge—like a game of connect-the-dots.

Hope gripped the seat beside her. Thank goodness she'd already arranged to look at used cars. She'd forgotten what an adventure riding with Gabby could be. "Is Tucker involved in this thing?"

Gabby leaned forward as she swerved toward another crater.

"He's in it right up to his neck, isn't he?" Hope persisted.

The road smoothed out, and Gabby sighed and settled back. "Honey, Shacktown was falling apart. That old factory was nothing but a hangout for winos, and it was getting so I hated to cross the bridge, even to go home." Waterside Apartments were on the east side of the river—the wrong side—but far enough north to have missed the stigma of being considered a part of Shacktown.

"In other words, he is." Hope answered her own question. She'd known it. There wasn't a reason in the world to suspect that a man who had grown up the way Tucker Owen had, whose fingernails had been black with grease more often than not, would be involved in a civic project with Princetown's elite, but he was. She'd had a funny feeling in the pit of her stomach ever since she'd stepped off that plane—like she wanted to turn around and run back to the safe obscurity of Boston.

Gabby passed a pickup truck doing forty-five and pulled back in front of him with inches to spare. "Whew! Slowpoke! Some drivers ought not to be allowed on the road."

"Gabby, why didn't you tell me about Tucker—that he was back in town—that he was involved in this business?"

"Maybe it never occurred to me you'd still be interested. I mean, you're the one who dumped him, not the other way around."

Hope remained silent. What could she say? That she hadn't dumped Tucker, as Gabby had so crudely put it—at least not willingly? How could she explain without sounding like a prize wimp that she'd only done what she had to do?

Hugh had been critically injured. His parents had said he was calling for her. Her parents had insisted on taking her to Boston to see him one last time, and once there, she'd been a pushover.

If only Tucker had needed her, even a little bit....

If only Hugh hadn't needed her quite so much....

"Well?" prompted Gabby, and Hope came to with a start to realize she'd been at it again—mired down in a past she had vowed to leave behind.

"I'm not 'still interested,' as you put it. It's just that—I mean, I only wanted to know— Oh, for goodness' sake, Gabby, there's nothing between Tucker and me. We were friends once, a long time ago. That's all."

"*All?* Ha! This is me, hon—the one you came crying to in the tenth grade, convinced you were pregnant because Tucker had put his tongue in your mouth." Gabby veered dangerously near the shoulder of the road as she stared at Hope. "You trying to tell me there was nothing going on between you two that last summer before you left for Boston? That week he took off from Atlanta and came home, and the two of you spent so much time down by the river?"

Hope felt the heat flood her face and she readjusted the air-conditioning vent. "Oh, for pity sake," she muttered.

"Honey, don't try to kid me. Even before that—back when we were in high school and Tucker was at Georgia Tech, and he'd take off for a weekend and race that old truck of his home, you two were generating enough voltage to light up River Ridge. All it took was seeing you two together—the whole town knew what was going on."

"Nothing was *going on*, as you put it," Hope snapped. "And anyway, that was years and years ago. I haven't seen or heard from him since."

Gabby lifted a glossy black brow. "You mean he never even sent you a wedding present?" She clicked her tongue until Hope felt like shaking her.

"Oh, shut up," Hope grumbled, and Gabby laughed.

"Okay, okay, but you may as well know that other women aren't so blind. Your loss is our gain."

"So I noticed," Hope said quietly, and when Gabby shot her a questioning look, she went on. "I saw him drive past the motel yesterday with this good-looking woman. Auburn hair, pretty face—she looked sort of familiar, but I couldn't place her. I wondered if— Well, I suppose he could be married by now."

"If he is, he sure hasn't let it cramp his style."

Hope didn't want to hear about it. Married or not, she didn't want to know about Tucker's conquests.

"Look, Hope, he's not married, all right? Not that he couldn't be if he wanted to, but you know what they say about buying a cow when milk's free."

"Huh?"

"No, I guess you wouldn't, would you? How about the one that says preachers' kids are the wildest kids in town? Have you heard that one?"

A little grimly, Hope laughed. "Only all my life."

"Yeah, well, you're the exception that proves the rule, as they say."

Hope subsided. She was no kid, wild or otherwise. She was a twenty-six-year old widow who, against her better judgment, had married a man she didn't love because he was dying, and both sets of parents, for reasons she still couldn't explain, had more or less pressured her into it.

"—so I'm just glad you finally got him out of your system," Gabby declared, and Hope realized she'd been drifting off into her own world again. She made an effort to put the past behind her as Gabby was saying, "—had the hots for that dude ever since we were in high school, but he was too busy playing nursemaid to you to look my way."

Hope gasped. "That's not true!"

"Anyway," Gabby continued, undeterred, "I'd hate like the devil to have to stand back and watch some other woman walk off with him. Of course, if the other woman was you,

I reckon I'd give him up. It would be a crime against nature, and that's the gospel truth.''

Gabby and Tucker? After the first stunned moment, Hope almost laughed aloud. It would be like pitting a yapping little terrier against a Doberman pinscher.

But there was no time to comment, because they were pulling into the parking lot of the new community center, and the first thing Hope saw was Tucker Owen standing on a makeshift platform scraping stickers off brand-new windowpanes.

The air rushed out of her lungs, leaving her feeling curiously deflated. Fortunately, Gabby was too busy retouching her mouth with Power Pink to notice.

He hadn't changed a bit. Yesterday she'd thought he looked older—tougher, if that were possible. But seeing him this way, his long back flaring up from a narrow waist to a pair of massive shoulders, and those powerful, denim-covered thighs swelling below his small, taut buttocks, she might have been sixteen years old all over again. Even her palms were sweating!

''Morning,'' sang out Gabby. Hope hung back, feeling suddenly gauche and colorless as she watched her friend hurry over to where Tucker was working, flashing brown legs, swirling white skirt, and cheerful chatter. Everything about Gabby seemed to sparkle.

Hope touched her own streaky blonde hair, which she'd worn in her usual French braid, tendrils slipping loose to tickle her face in the humid heat. Suddenly, it seemed so drab compared with dark, flyaway curls. In her beige shirtwaister, she was all one color—invisible.

Tucker laid his scraper on the window ledge. He had heard the car drive up and seen the reflection of the two women. There was no way he could fail to recognize her. He would have known her if their paths had crossed in the dead of night on a side street in Bombay.

Damn her soul! Why couldn't she have stayed away? Why did she have to come back now and stir things up, just when he was beginning to get it all together again? And what the hell was she doing in this part of town, anyway—slumming?

He had dropped Josie off the night before at 10:20, pleading a migraine, which hadn't been far from the truth. She had given him a look he hadn't dared try to decipher and said, "I heard Hope Outlaw—Phillips, I guess she is now—was back in town. For a kid with all the personality of a wet vanilla wafer, she did all right for herself, didn't she? Poor old Hugh was a prime jerk, but I guess if you're rich enough, it doesn't matter."

Slumming, he decided now as he watched her without seeming to. Or maybe like all those other lady Ridgebacks who'd been swarming around lately, she had come to make a donation of an hour or two of her valuable time between golf lessons and bridge luncheons.

"Hey, Tucker, in case I forgot to mention it in my résumé, I don't do windows," Gabby carolled up at him.

Reluctantly, Tucker dropped to the ground. "Gabby, glad you could make it." And after a barely perceptible pause, "Hello, Hope, nice to see you again." He was reasonably confident that nothing of what he was feeling would show on his face. He'd had plenty of practice over the years in concealing his emotions.

"So...here we are. Bring on the kids!" Gabby said brightly.

Tucker forced himself to smile. "I hope you know what you're letting yourself in for. Ever since that piece came out in the paper Sunday, my phone's been ringing off the hook with women wanting to know when they can unload on us. C'mon, I'll give you the grand tour." His face felt stiff, but he forced a smile that wouldn't have convinced a dead man. "Uh, Hope—you want to join us? Or you can wait in the lobby—we've already got it furnished. It's through there...."

Gesturing, he willed her to get out of his sight, out of his building, out of his town—before his thin veneer of manners cracked and he said what was on his mind.

"Hey, this is great!" Gabby cried enthusiastically. They were standing just inside the wide double doorway, on the newly refinished locust floors, their varying levels joined by low ramps instead of steps. "What a place for a skateboard!"

Tearing his attention away from Hope, Tucker forced himself to begin telling her about the various groups that had signed up for space. "We'll have a public health nurse come in regularly on a weekly schedule, we've got a social worker, some art people from the community college, and...lemme see, there's something about canning and preserving coming up right soon, and we're looking into finding someone to teach sewing and furniture repair. I've got some bands lined up for dances if we can get chaperons and sponsors. Something for the kids, you know? I reckon we'll sort of pick up momentum as we go...leastwise, I'm sure hoping so."

From the corner of his eye, Tucker caught a glimpse of Hope. She was standing primly in the middle of the corridor with her hands clasped in front of her, exactly the way she used to do when she was feeling threatened or insecure.

His blue eyes turned the color of slate. "If you've seen enough here, I'll show you the area I had in mind for the care center."

"You coming, Hope? You're in this thing as deep as I am." Gabby waited for Hope to catch up with them. Eyes narrowed, Tucker led them into an enormous room that had been painted the palest shade of peach—rafters, braces, steam pipes and all.

What the hell did she mean—Hope was in this thing as deeply as she was?

But he knew. God, what a fool he'd been not to have figured it out before now! It had been staring him in the face all along, but he'd wanted it not to be true—willed it not to be true.

His eyes were like polished flint by the time he swiveled them around to where Hope stood hesitantly just inside the room. She was watching him the way a trapped kitten would watch a pit bull, and he felt no sympathy at all. "You want to tell me what the hell you think you're trying to pull here, Hope?" he asked with a quiet emphasis that isolated the two of them on a cold, desolate planet.

"Well, I—that is, I wasn't trying to—to pull anything."

"No? This is not your idea of a joke, then?"

She straightened up until her eyes were on a level with his chin. "Certainly not. I needed a job. Gabby needed someone to go in with her, and I—well, it just seemed like a natural. I don't see why you're getting so upset about it now— You knew, didn't you?"

"Knew!"

She flinched as the word exploded from him. "You're on the committee, aren't you? Why wouldn't you know? And stop looking at me as if I were trying to sabotage your precious center! We have a contract—"

"Which I hereby declare invalid!"

"You can't. Gabby signed it and so did George Harrington. And anyway, I don't see what you have against me, but whatever it is—"

"Don't you?" His voice suddenly turned silky, and Hope shivered.

Gabby stepped between them. "Hey, look, tiger, we can hash out any differences you two have between you later, okay? Right now I want to see where we'll be working, and I don't have all day."

She might as well not have been there for all the attention they paid her. In a louder voice, she tried again. "Now, you listen here, Tucker Owen, you might have set yourself up as lord and mayor of Shacktown, but George down at the bank signed us both to a year's contract—with options! And what's more, he gave us the authority to hire on a part-timer, subject to his approval, and he didn't say word one about checking first with you, so you might as well stop all your huffing and puffing, okay?''

Gabby was doing some huffing of her own by the time she wound down, but Tucker made a valiant effort to control his own breathing and his explosive temper. He glanced at Hope, ashamed of his outburst. She was so white her eyes looked like craters. Even her lips were pale, and he felt like a damned dog, which made him angry all over again.

Why did he let her get to him this way? He was old enough to know better. Dammit, he was acting exactly the way he had twenty years ago whenever he ran up against a stone wall. Which was about every day of his life. Go find the biggest, toughest jerk around, pick a fight and then knock the stuffing out of him.

"Okay?" Gabby insisted, pushing her face up at him.

Tucker cleared his throat. "Yeah—sorry. Okay."

He would wait her out. She wouldn't last a week. Nothing in her sheltered background had ever equipped her for the conditions she would face down here. Hunger. Abuse. Desertion. Decent people doing their damnedest to make it on next to nothing, and the scum who preyed on them for the little they had.

He gestured to the freshly painted walls. Scowling, he said, "If you don't like the color, you can change it, but you'll have to hustle the paint yourself. I've already hit on every paint dealer from Wake Forest to Rocky Mount."

Gabby sashayed over to examine the view from the outside doors, and Tucker stole a glance at Hope to see if she was all right. When their eyes tangled and clung for an interminable moment, he wished he'd let well enough alone.

Tucker was standing in a pose Hope remembered all too well—shoulders hunched, feet spread apart as if braced for trouble, thumbs hooked into the loops of his jeans. He seldom wore a belt. He wasn't wearing one now. As old memories swarmed over her, she felt a film of perspiration bead her face, and she fumbled in her purse for her handkerchief as she crossed the room to stand at a window.

Handkerchiefs. Silly little scraps of cloth, with embroidered flowers or lace trim. She was the only woman Tucker had ever met besides his mother who used handkerchiefs instead of tissues.

"This used to be the receiving area," he said, and she stiffened as if she hadn't heard him follow her. Moccasins didn't make a whole lot of noise. "I walled up part of the doorway and turned the loading dock into a deck. That stretch out there I thought would make a good playground—we can haul in a load of sand or whatever you need and get some play stuff."

"That's Hope's department. When it comes to playground equipment, I'm an expert on inner-tube floats, tires hung up from trees, and horses made from evaporated milk cans that clamp onto your shoes, with rope bridles." Gabby spoke from behind him, and resenting her presence, Tucker forced himself to step back and include her.

"Oh, well, I . . ." Hope began, but he was pushed to the wall by the way her nearness affected him.

"Yeah, I'm sure you want to help out, Hope, but the truth is, this isn't really going to be your kind of place. Anyhow, I expect you'll be going back up north again pretty soon, won't you?"

Eyes sparkling, Hope opened her mouth to reply when once again, Gabby stepped in between them.

"Wow, this place is perfect, Tucker. Indestructible walls, indestructible floors—they can really cut loose here. Thank the Lord I'll be holed up in my nice, quiet little office when all hell breaks loose." At his blank look, she said, "You *did* remember to set aside a place for a desk, a chair, a filing cabinet and maybe a microwave, didn't you?"

"Oh, sure. That is, you've got my permission to slice up the space anyway you want to. Uh—is there all that much office work involved in baby-sitting?"

"Baby-sitting! Look, I don't know whether Congress is going to settle for refunds or tax credits or what, but you can bet your booties that whenever our government gets mixed up in any project, there's going to be seventeen million miles of red tape involved. I wouldn't open a worm ranch without complete records of every single transaction from day one."

Feeling thoroughly chastened, Tucker grinned and said, "Yeah—well, speaking of transactions, how about figuring out what you're going to be needing in the way of playground equipment? Bunch of the guys down at the Charlotte Speedway last week said they'd ante up for the heavy duty stuff."

"That's Hope's department. I'll handle the paperwork involved. When it comes to filling out forms, I'm your woman," she said with an undercurrent of something strictly off-the-record in her tone.

Hope braced herself to get involved in the discussion, but she was never given the chance. Hooking his arm through Gabby's, Tucker steered her out onto the deck. "Yeah, but you'll be the one to order what we need and clear it through the finance committee. They're not paying, but they have to know anyway. You record keepers are all alike. Come on, let me show you the size of the playground and maybe you can get a handle on how much we're going to need to spend."

At the last minute, Gabby turned back and said, "Hope? This is where you come in."

Tucker shrugged as if he didn't care one way or the other. "Sure, come along if you're interested." Seeing her lift her head the way she used to when some of the older kids started ragging her, he felt a wash of guilt and fought it down. He'd done nothing to feel guilty about, he told himself. She was trying to butt in where she didn't belong, that was all. Where she wasn't wanted.

"I can see well enough from here, thanks," Hope said quietly. "Will we have the entire fenced area?"

"Half of it. The other side will be a basketball court for the older kids."

"I'd better see what shape that fence is in," Gabby said. "And while we're at it, how about insurance?"

Hope remained in the doorway, looking as aloof as an angel on top of a tree. Tucker still felt like a dog, and he didn't care for the feeling one bit. Standing in the shade of an awning donated by a local businessman, he studiously avoided looking back, but even so, the image of Hope's deceptively fragile features lingered in his mind.

How well he remembered the set of that stubborn little chin. The first time he'd come to her rescue, when she was being tormented by a pack of eighth grade boys, she'd been standing there with her hands clasped in front of her and her chin thrust out that same way, as if she could hold them off by sheer force of will.

With scrapes on both her knees and the sash of her silly ruffled dress dangling, she'd been scared stiff and trying so damned hard not to show it, that he'd wanted to wrap her in cotton wool and tuck her into the silver-colored box along with the plastic angel his mother used to save for the top of the Christmas tree, back when they'd bothered to have one.

And dammit, against all reason, he still felt the same way!

The examination of the chain-link fence took only a few minutes, although Gabby seemed determined to drag it out. Tucker was amused. She was an attractive little thing. Brash as a blue jay, but likable, and damned capable, from all reports. He happened to know that she hadn't had anything handed to her on a silver platter, like some women he could name. He had checked out her background as soon as her name had come up, and learned that she'd known the meaning of hard work from the time she was big enough to toddle along between rows of tobacco.

But what he admired about her most of all was the way she'd taken up with a scared kid whose folks didn't have any better sense than to dress her up in ruffles, ribbons and ringlets and send her off to school with orders to mind the teachers and be a good little girl.

It had been Gabby who had taken Hope in hand and showed her how to tuck in the ruffles and do something else with her hair once she got to school. It had been Gabby who had showed her how to use lipstick and eye shadow when they were in their teens, but it had been Hope who had got the licking for it. He remembered the day she'd come running to meet him, crying because her folks had ordered her to keep away from Gabby Boger.

God knows what they would have said if they'd known she was meeting Tucker down by the river every chance she got, and pouring out her heart to him.

She'd told him everything in those days—about how much she wanted to be allowed to dress like the other girls, and go out on dates, and work someplace besides Eula Finley's day-care center.

She'd told him when she got her first period. He'd known she was hurting, and figured it out, anyway. He'd told her a damned sight more about what went on with a woman's body than her old lady had ever bothered to explain, and since Mrs. Outlaw had signed a request that Hope be excused from sex-education class, such as it was in those days, there'd been a hell of a lot she'd needed to learn.

And he'd taught her. God, yes, he'd taught her. And he'd fully expected to go on teaching her and protecting her and taking care of her for the rest of his life. But first he'd had to get his degree, because Preacher Outlaw was real big on degrees. After that, he'd planned to find a good job with room for advancement, put a down payment on a nice place over on the west side of the river, and then speak to her parents before he gave her a ring.

Oh, yeah, he'd had it all planned out. He'd about gone crazy, wanting her so bad, but determined to wait until things could be perfect for them. He'd planned to surprise her with it at Christmas—the lot he'd picked out, his plans for their future—the ring. Only before he had a chance to get a few days off from the job that had put him through school, she'd gone off and got herself married to a Ridgeback wimp!

"So what about it, Tucker?"

"Huh?" He realized that Gabby had been tugging at his arm for some time. Actually, tugging wasn't precisely the word to describe the motions of her small, square hands on his arm, but he was in no mood to encourage her.

"I said what if we talk about it some more over steaks at my place this evening? I'll do some checking around and have some figures ready for you by then."

Tucker glanced at the doorway. Hope was nowhere in sight. Evidently, she'd gotten tired of waiting and wandered off. Now if she'd been the one to ask him, he might have....

No, dammit, he'd have needed his head examined to get involved again.

"How about it? I'll even scrape the rust off my grill for the occasion. That'll give you some idea of how seriously I take my work."

Tucker looked down on the headful of dark, curly hair. She met his eyes with frank appraisal, letting him know without words that she was more than willing to further their acquaintance if he was game.

Black eyes, olive skin that tanned to a richness that was probably unhealthy, but looked damned good—she was a little too brash to suit his taste, but if he had a grain of sense, he'd take her up on her implied offer.

The trouble was, he kept running head-on into a pale oval face with a scattering of coppery freckles, a wealth of hair that felt like silk and smelled like honeysuckle, and a pair of eyes that could see right through to the inside of his soul.

"Yeah, sure—why not?" he said suddenly, feeling an inexplicable tightness in the region of his solar plexus.

Three

————

Tucker was having second thoughts even before he reached the street where the Waterside Apartments complex was located. By the time he reached the small cluster of redwood units, he was ready to turn tail and run.

Tucker had never run from a fight in his life, regardless of the odds. He liked fighting—had never minded being overmatched. But this was different. While the woman hadn't exactly come on to him today, she'd managed to let him know that if he was interested in exploring the possibilities, she was game.

Not that she'd been brazen, but a man could sense these things. And when the feeling wasn't mutual, it could be pretty damned uncomfortable. Especially when the couple in question was involved in a business relationship.

And *most* especially when the other woman in the relationship happened to be the one woman in all the world Tucker had ever come close to loving.

Close—! Hell, he'd practically worshiped Hope! Even after seven years, all she had to do was look at him and he was right back where he'd been then—a ham-handed kid with a smart mouth and no manners, with too much pride and not enough money—a kid who had seen more ugliness in his first dozen years than she could imagine in a lifetime.

And if she thought for one minute that he was going to let her come down to Shacktown and play lady—if she thought he'd stand by and watch her exposing herself to punks like Billy Coe and the gang that hung out at J.J.'s Billiards just down the street, she could damned well think again! Hope wouldn't last a week over here.

Tucker raked a hand through his hair, secured his shirt-tail inside his beltless jeans, and climbed the steps to 24-B. Why the devil had he agreed to come here tonight? He was in no mood to make conversation, much less anything else, he told himself as he took the stairs two at a time.

With any luck he could make it through a simple dinner date and escape without involving himself in anything sticky. Although strictly speaking, Gabby Boger wasn't even a date. She was a business acquaintance.

Hope answered the door. She stood there before him, dark eyes enormous in the pale oval of her face. Wearing a flowery dress with a lacy collar, she looked both vulnerable and untouchable, and Tucker felt something hard and cold inside him begin to crumble.

"Gabby didn't say anything about you being here." The words were almost an accusation, and he thought he saw her wince, but she recovered so quickly he decided he had imagined it.

"I'm not. Here, I mean. That is, I'm leaving—I have to go out." Despite her tangled tongue, her voice was cool.

He gave her a look that bordered on the scornful. *This is me, Tucker, you're talking to, girl. Don't look at me like butter wouldn't melt in your mouth, because I know better. I know just how hot and greedy that little mouth of yours can be!*

"Gabby's in the shower. She'll be out in a minute, and you're to make yourself at home." With a graciousness born of her "yes, ma'am, thank you, ma'am" background, she stood aside for him to enter.

Tucker felt all the old resentments begin to simmer in him again, and he fought them to a standstill. He'd come a long way since those days—she was no more to him now than any other woman he'd gone out with a few times. Less, actually—what they'd shared had been kid stuff. It had meant little enough to her—it meant still less to him.

Not wanting to appear empty-handed, Tucker had brought along a bottle of red burgundy, considering it a step up from candy, but less personal than flowers. Now he wished he'd brought all three—or nothing at all. He shoved the brown bag into Hope's hand with a muttered reference to the weather and turned to stare at a colorful bullfighting poster.

He could feel her behind him, feel a familiar tension begin to gather in his body. He wanted to tell her she didn't have to hang around on his account, but all he could think of was how much she had changed.

And how much she hadn't. Her eyes were still the same shade of melting brown, but they seemed larger somehow. There were shadows there now that he didn't recall from the past. Although her face had a maturity that was new, her skin still held the dewy softness that made him want to touch it.

Against his will, he began remembering the way she had once burned in his arms—the way her cheeks had flushed with sexual heat when he had held her, tempted almost beyond the point of no return.

She was a woman now, he reminded himself. That would explain the changes—that unusual air of calmness that wasn't precisely calmness, but more a waiting quality, as if she'd been waiting for something a long time. And was willing to wait forever.

Expelling his breath in a sharp gust, he turned once more to glare at the poster, his head full of warnings and self-recriminations. Remember, he told himself, you're here about the day-care facility in the community center, and that's *all* you're here for! Two solid years you've worked your tail off on this project, and you're *not* going to screw up now on account of some frosty little blonde.

You don't have a damn thing to prove to anyone—not anymore. If you owe any woman anything, it's your mother—not Hope. It's the woman who found herself pregnant with you thirty-one years ago and was forced to marry a man who wasn't worth the dirt on the soles of her shoes. Not a woman who dumped a man at the first glitter of another man's gold.

Yeah, he didn't have to prove anything to any woman, Tucker told himself. So how come all he could do was stand here and sweat over the way Hope's skin looked in the lamplight? How come all he could think of was the way it had once looked with the late-afternoon sun shining down on skin it had never shone on before—the delicate pale hollow of her belly—when she lay trembling beneath him, begging him to make her a woman—his woman?

With a rough gesture, Tucker wiped the film of sweat from his forehead. Unbidden, a picture of Hugh Phillips's slender, manicured hands on that milk-white body swam before his eyes, and he wanted to hit out at something...hard!

"Hey, Tucker, sorry I'm running late," Gabby called out from the bathroom. "If you're any sort of a hand with fires, how about getting the charcoal started? Hope can show you where everything is."

The bathroom door slammed shut, and for a moment, neither of them moved. And then Hope murmured, "If you'll just come this way."

He could have shaken her. Where the hell did she get off, speaking to him as if he were just some guy she'd called in to unclog her sink or something? As if she'd never laid eyes on him before?

She'd laid a hell of a lot more on him than her eyes, and perversely, he didn't want her to forget it. "A real grill, huh? Not like the old days down on the river, is it?"

They had built small fires on the ground and roasted wieners and marshmallows and fed them to each other, the eating, laughing and finger-licking always leading to something more. Now his smile held more than an edge of cruelty as he turned to see the perceptible lift of her head.

On the defense again. She remembered, all right.

"You probably want to remove the cover from the grill," she said as calmly as if he hadn't just hit her where she lived.

Go ahead, duchess, spread it on—I happen to know that underneath those Sunday School manners of yours there's a trembling little girl who used to be afraid of her own shadow until a guy named Tucker came along and made her forget everything but his arms, his kisses—his way of loving her.

"The charcoal is under there. I believe it's the self-starting kind, but there's fluid, too, if you need it."

Had Phillips been any good for her? Had he been able to wipe out the memory of those sweet summer afternoons down by the river, when they hadn't quite gone all the way, but had gone far enough so that he would never—*could* never—forget it?

"I'm afraid I don't know where the matches are. Probably in the..." Hope turned then and met his gaze, the acid of old memories hot between them. She took several quick gulps of air, and then she said, "Tucker, I don't want to—that is, I'd better leave. I'm going...right now. I only wanted to let you in, but..."

Her voice dwindled off to a whisper, and Tucker knew a moment of fierce satisfaction in realizing that she was no more immune than he was. He could still get to her—he made her nervous.

She got to him, too. She made him hot as a firecracker, and mad as hell. It was a start, he told himself. A start that was going nowhere if he had anything to do with it.

They stared at one another, Tucker's slate-gray eyes pinning her to the wall. He could feel the muscles in his jaw working, and he made a conscious effort to relax. At this rate, he'd have a splitting headache in no time—which might not be such a bad idea. At least he'd have an excuse to cut this fiasco short.

Tension shimmered between them, sucking out all the stifling, humid air on the tiny second-floor balcony. *Don't do this to me, dammit! Go back where you belong and leave me alone! Pink-and-yellow angels belong on Christmas trees, not down here in the real world.*

"Hey, nice wine! Real cork and everything. What's the holdup?"

"Matches," Hope blurted.

"Gabby," Tucker said, "maybe we ought to give it a few days—you haven't had time to get together any kind of information yet. I've been going in high gear for so long, I forget that not everyone has the same interest in the center that I do."

Gabby, smelling of Obsession perfume and glittering with gold eye shadow and copper lip gloss, jangled an armful of bracelets in a gesture of dismissal. "Quit racing your engine, sugar—I've had all afternoon, haven't I? What do you think the yellow pages are for?"

"Yes, but—"

"So I've got three bids already, sight unseen, and two more good leads."

"Bids!" Tucker gawked at her. "What the devil did you get bids on? We haven't even figured out what we need yet."

She shrugged, and Hope murmured an excuse and slipped inside the apartment. "I simply told them I was getting ready to open a day-care place, with a view to franchising later on, and said I wasn't quite satisfied with the dealer that had been recommended. Then I asked what their rock-bottom price would be to supply me with a minimum of top-of-the-line equipment. Nothing in writing on either side yet, but it's a starting place. Most of those kids would be thrilled with a tractor tire slung up into a sycamore tree, and a mudslide down a creekbank.''

''Which they already have,'' Tucker said with a glimmer of amusement. ''Franchising! You're a real little hustler, you know that?'' He edged closer to the door in an effort to see where Hope had gone. ''How do you know we can afford top of the line?''

''You said the guys at the speedway were kicking in. They know the value of decent equipment. Besides, we need it for insurance. It never pays to skimp where liability suits are a possibility.''

''Maybe Hope could...'' That was as far as he got before he saw Hope cross the living room, open the front door, and close it quietly behind her.

''I'll go over figures with you before I actually go see any of these clowns,'' Gabby was saying while he stared at the white paneled door. She removed the bag of charcoal from Tucker's unresisting hands, and disregarding her yellow gauze dress, dumped it onto the grill, blowing away a cloud of black dust. ''She's still got to collect her things from the motel, and she wanted to drive by the parsonage and take a look for old times' sake. Then, while she was over that way, she planned to drop in on Miss Eula, and that could take all night. That woman can evermore talk!''

The valley was layered with bands of copper and magenta mist, which seemed to grow duller even as Tucker watched. He didn't kid himself about the reason, and as a result of his self-disgust, he made a deliberate effort to be a charming guest.

''Here, give me those matches,'' he commanded masterfully. ''You'll get your hands dirty.''

Four and a half hours later, Tucker let himself inside his own house. He'd left a lamp burning in the living room because he'd always hated coming home to a dark house. More often than not, it had been not only dark, but damp and cheerless—cold in winter, hot in summer, and smelling musty and old at the best of times.

He had changed all that, even though it was too late to do his mother any good. As for the old man, he had finally completed the job of drinking himself to death when Tucker was about eighteen. It had been the only job he'd ever finished, Tuck thought with a bitterness that had softened little over the years.

He was comfortably tired. They had talked business and local politics, and somewhat to his surprise, Gabby hadn't pushed the personal angle. Maybe she'd noticed the way he'd reacted when Hope had left. Maybe he wasn't as good an actor as he'd thought.

The steaks had been great, the salad all right if you liked that kind of stuff. She had fancied up a pair of potatoes with cheese and green things sprinkled all over the top, but they'd tasted okay. He'd limited himself to one glass of wine, and she'd finished off the rest. For her size, she could really put it away. Not a particularly attractive trait in anyone, to Tucker's way of thinking—especially in a woman. Still, her work record was flawless. Evidently, she could handle it.

He hated to admit that he'd hung around just on the off chance that Hope would come back. Not until it had finally dawned on him that she wasn't coming in as long as his car was in the parking lot, had he made his excuses and left.

Hope had collected her two big suitcases and assorted tote bags and driven by the parsonage. The shutters had been given a fresh coat of paint, and her father's roses were thriving. He had set them out himself, and tended them as if they were a part of his flock. She made a mental note to write him that they looked better than ever this summer, in spite of the drought.

After that she had driven out to Miss Eula's house and stayed on until nearly nine-thirty. They had supper to-

gether, and the garrulous old woman had given her the
benefit of thirty-seven years of child-care wisdom before
starting in to catch her up on the news of the past few years.

Among other things, Hope had learned that the Owen
boy had turned out better than anyone ever thought he
would. He'd worked his way through engineering school
and then taken over Ziglar Motors when old man Ziglar had
a stroke, and done right well for himself, considering what
he had come from—although Mollie Tucker had been from
a decent, God-fearing family before she'd gotten mixed up
with the likes of Jimmy Owen.

Why, Miss Eula remembered as it it were yesterday, the
very morning Mollie had been called out of class to the
principal's office, and the next thing everyone knew, she'd
been married to that shiftless Gin-Jim Owen, and her as
pregnant as a pea pod!

Her folks had washed their hands of her. Bought the
house over across the bridge for them, and then moved
away, some said all the way to Southport.

Feeling guilty at listening to all this ancient gossip, most
of which she had already heard, Hope tried tactfully to
change the subject. "I drove past the parsonage on my way
here. The roses look great, don't they? Daddy will be so
pleased someone's looking after them."

"That's Sally Jemison. She helps out there a couple days
a week. Never had a speck of leaf-spot in all the years I can
remember. You remember Sally, don't you? Her father has
that pool hall down on the corner of Pokeberry and Second?"

Hope remembered J.J.'s Billiards, all right. Tucker had
told her it was a hangout for the toughest element in town,
and he should know. He'd once claimed he could eat for a
week on what he could pick up in a single afternoon there
at the tables. She hadn't known what he meant, and he'd
had to explain the fine art of hustling pool, and then he'd
warned her that if he ever caught her within a country mile

of the place, he would take her to her daddy and see that he whomped the living daylights out of her.

Oh, for pity sake! Why did everything always have to remind her of Tucker Owen?

Miss Eula walked her to the front gate, and Hope commented on the old oak and the way the yard had improved now that the children no longer trampled through it like a herd of elk. They inhaled the mingled scents of honeysuckle, grape blossoms and Rosa multiflora while fireflies swooped high up in the treetops.

Miss Eula said it meant no rain for three days. "Lawsy, we sure could use some. You come back now, y'hear?"

"I'll do that, Miss Eula. And thanks for all your advice. I'll probably be calling on you for more once we get started."

"Pshaw, you'll be too busy to think about an old relic like me. That Owen boy did a real nice thing, buying up that old factory and donating it to the community." Which was the first Hope had ever heard of Tucker's role in the project. "You tell him Miss Eula said he turned out real fine—real fine, mmm-hmm."

Hope's new car, an elderly Honda, stalled twice before she managed to get away. After each false start, she waved and smiled at the woman who stood under the yellow bug light on the front porch. She seriously doubted if she would be passing on Miss Eula's message to Tucker, but she felt warm all over, just hearing it. There had been a time not so long ago when no one on this side of the river had had a kind word to say for the son of the town drunkard. She had wondered even then if they were all blind, because she'd been able to see the good in him right from the very first.

Gabby was asleep when she let herself in, the dishes piled haphazardly in the sink to be rinsed, and the wine bottle empty.

It must have been a successful evening, Hope thought as she unpacked her suitcases in the tiny room that had served as a storage place, and which was now Hope's bedroom. She placed two photographs of her parents on a scarred oak desk—one taken at their church in Weaverville and another at a mission in Central America. Next, she arranged her brush and mirror alongside them. She yawned, and after spreading a sheet over the new mattress, was asleep almost before her head hit the pillow.

For the next week, Hope was busy dealing with various workmen on such matters as partitions and plumbing. In the evenings she would scribble away at lists and drawings, tired from the day at the center, but eager to get back again.

There were always several interested bystanders, anxious to know when they could come and play basketball or get their blood pressure checked, or leave their children with someone reliable while they worked or looked for work.

A half-grown boy who reminded Hope of a young Tucker was one of the more persistent. "Hey, you a nurse or somep'in?" he asked that first day.

Hope had a vague feeling that she knew him, or at least that she'd seen him somewhere before. "Sorry. Just a would-be baby-sitter. I'm going to be working in the child-care area once we get it finished."

"Oh." A bit self-consciously, he prowled around the large room, looking distinctly out of place against the pale peach walls. He had Tucker's coloring, except for the eyes, but other than that, the resemblance was more in attitude than anything else—the same tough-guy stance that was too pronounced to be quite real, at least in someone so young. Despite his gawky height and the breadth of his shoulders in the ragged T-shirt with the vulgar slogan on the back, Hope thought he couldn't be much more than fourteen.

"Do you play basketball?" she asked, putting aside the catalog of stencils she hoped to use to brighten up the barren walls.

"Nah, 'at's kid stuff. Hey, you live around here or somep'in?"

"I used to. At least, over across the river." Either the boy was blushing or he had an overdose of sun, and with that tan of his, she didn't see how that was possible.

"Oh, yeah...thought you looked like one o' them Ridgebacks." He sauntered toward the door, where he'd left his skateboard, and acting purely on impulse, Hope called him back.

"You wouldn't happen to know of anyone's who's good at painting pictures on walls, would you?"

His long neck swiveled around, and he gave her a suspicious look. "You kiddin', lady? Hey, I don't do that kind of stuff, 'n' anybody says I do is lyin', you hear?"

"My name is Hope Phillips, and nobody said you did anything. I've got some ideas about how these walls should look, but I can't seem to find the right stencils. Anyway, I'm not even sure stencils would work on such a rough surface." The main support walls, as well as the outer ones, were of rough, painted brick.

He stared at her for a moment, and she could have sworn she saw a glimmer of interest in his dark, intelligent eyes, but then he just shrugged, scooped up his skateboard and left.

Hope winced at the sound of wheels on Tucker's newly finished hardwood floors. Once the place was overrun with senior citizens and toddlers, they just might have a small problem.

Tucker deliberately stayed away from the center, knowing that Hope was there every day now. There was plenty to do at work—he'd finished redesigning a racing fuel bowl that would eliminate a lot of the problems that had arisen with the old-style carburetors, and now it was being installed on three of the cars that would be competing at the First Union 500 at North Wilkesboro. After the race he would be talking to several manufacturers, two of whom were already producing products he had designed.

"Bucky's a positive, and Dale says he'll try to make it," Evelyn called out.

"Earnhardt or Jarrett?" Tucker groaned as he tried to straighten up from his drafting table. He'd forgotten exactly how many race drivers he'd invited to the opening. So near the fourth of July, most of them had other commitments.

"Earnhardt. Ned'll be in Daytona, but I've got a call in for Richard. You want me to see if we can get Kyle, too? And how about Bob and Davey?"

Shoving back the forelock that had fallen over his forehead, Tucker strolled into his secretary's office. "What d'you think this is, father and son day?" With the center all but finished, Tucker had been spending most of his spare time planning a bang-up all-day opening, short on ceremony, long on fun. He wanted to get as many people there as possible, from both sides of the river, but mostly, he wanted the citizens of Shacktown to feel that this was their center.

Because it was. He had done all he could do—the rest was up to the community. They could accept it or reject it.

"Go home, Tucker. You've got a headache already, haven't you?"

"Bull. Quit trying to henpeck me, I'm not your husband. I'm your employer—at the moment."

Evelyn showed her opinion of that remark with a ladylike snort, which Tucker ignored. They could go on this way forever.

"You get in touch with County General?" he asked tiredly.

"They'll have an ambulance and crew on standby, and they're going to set up a display with handouts on everything from tick bites to tonsillitis." She shuffled through her notes. "Oh, and by the way, the barbecue people want to set up the day before. They're figuring two sides of beef and a hundred fifty pounds of pork, with the usual trimmings. Once they get the firebox put together and the coals going, they'll start cooking. They're aiming to start serving no later than eleven, because once people get a whiff, they're apt to stampede.''

''Maybe we'd better keep the medics on the other side of the building. We don't want anybody thinking about cholesterol when they line up for that second plateful. Might be the only meal some of 'em will have all day. Oh, and see about getting some bags, will you? The kind they can take home leftovers in. And order another side of beef and a few more hams, while you're at it.''

''Do you have the slightest idea what all this is going to cost you?''

''No, and I'd appreciate it if you wouldn't tell me, either.''

Standing before a window that looked out on a row of newly renovated mill houses, a project he had pushed, but not invested money in, Tucker flexed the tired muscles of his back. He'd been bent over the drafting table for the past three hours, and over an experimental 3.5 liter, six-hundred horse engine for a few more than that.

Evelyn had been right. He had a headache. But then, what else was new? She'd made two appointments for him to have his eyes examined, and he'd managed to miss both of them. Not deliberately, of course, although she'd never believed him.

Hell, he was getting old. Sometimes he thought he'd been born old.

When the phone rang, Tucker had been asleep just long enough so that it took him several seconds to cut through the fog. His heart did a few slam-dunks before he remembered that a call in the middle of the night no longer meant that he had to go bail his old man out of the tank, or clean him up and haul him home from Greasy's Tavern—hopefully without waking his mother.

''Yeah, who'sis?'' he mumbled, lying flat on his back, naked under the lazily spinning ceiling fan.

''Sa'jint Ellis down to the po-lice station. We picked up the Coe kid again. Got a call, some jerk had set fire to them tires out behind the Exxon next to Proctor's Hardware. Kid claims he didn't have nothing to do with it, but they caught him hanging around, brought him in for questioning.''

"What time is it?''

"Now, you mean? Uh—twenty-two and a half past three.''

Tucker uttered a short vulgarity and rolled out of bed. In a weak moment, he'd told Chief Conners to let him know if Billy got in trouble again, but dammit, he'd thought he'd straightened the kid out when he'd got him that part-time summer job.

"Hang on, I'll be there in ten minutes,'' he muttered.

"Sorry to bother you, Tuck. You busy or something?''

"Oh, hell no, I wasn't doing a damned thing but trying to sleep!''

Billy was sullen and Tucker was disgusted when he slammed out of the station with the kid in tow. He was in no mood to listen to protestations of innocence. "I told you if you screwed up again I was through,'' he snarled, shoving the tight-faced youth out the door ahead of him.

"I didn't do nothing,'' Billy muttered.

"What the hell were you doing out at this time of night?''

"My old lady had a friend in. I ain't staying around and listening to—''

Like everyone else in the neighborhood, Tucker knew that Wanda Coe had been entertaining a lot lately—especially late at night. A woman alone had a living to make, but hell—! "All right, so you could have come over to my place.''

"Yeah, sure, and get sent up for breakin' and enterin'!''

"You want a key?''

"Hell no, I don't want a key! I don't need no—''

Tucker shut him up before he talked himself in any deeper. Not for the first time, he wondered why he bothered. Billy wasn't the first kid he'd bailed out of trouble, but he was the one who kept right on jumping back in.

Okay, so he knew why he bothered. Wanda had been there for his mother when she was sick, and Tucker had needed all the help he could get. He owed her for that. Besides, the kid reminded him a little too much of himself at that age. Tucker hadn't had anyone to turn to, and God knows he could have used a role model back then.

But he'd had something even better. He'd had a wide-eyed, squeaky-clean kid who had looked up at him one day and smiled through her tears, and something had happened to him. From that day on, he'd been determined not to let her down.

And he hadn't. Not even after he'd found out that she'd run off and married that sonofabitch her parents had kept cramming down her throat. He'd gotten drunk, and then he'd gotten into a fight—damned near killed some poor jerk just because he happened to be wearing the wrong kind of clothes and came from the right side of the river.

After that, he'd straightened up and gone ahead with his plans as if his world hadn't fallen down around his ears.

Because from the time he'd been sixteen years old, Tucker had had his future all mapped out. He'd had his goals. Number one, he was going to be his own boss, no matter how long it took. Something to do with engines, because even then, he'd never seen an engine he couldn't take apart and put back together so that it worked a hell of a lot better. It was a God-given talent, and he wasn't about to let it go to waste.

Goal number two—he was going to get the hell out of Shacktown. Out of Princetown and maybe even out of North Carolina. He was going to head for a place where no one had ever heard of Shacktown, or Mollie Tucker, who had got herself in trouble and had to marry Gin-Jim Owen, who had drunk himself to death at the glorious age of thirty-five, just a few years older than Tucker was now.

Okay, so he hadn't done too well on that one. He'd gone, all right, but he hadn't stayed. It had come to him somewhere along the line that a guy couldn't run away from himself, so he'd quit trying.

And then there'd been goal number three. He smiled a little grimly as he remembered that one. Goal number three: marry Hope Outlaw.

Four

Sitting in her father's old church on Sunday morning, Hope lost herself in the scent of lemon oil and roses, the sound of Dr. Saunders's sonorous voice and the sight of sunlight streaming down through the stained glass windows to spill out over the congregation. As a child, she used to entertain herself during her father's sermons by picking out blue faces with orange noses, and the elderly men whose white hair had magically turned all colors of the rainbow.

There'd been a time when the confetti of colored light had been amusing. Now she found it soothing. Reassuring—a part of her life that had not changed. The deepest notes of the organ stirred to life, sending a familiar vibration along her spine as the choir launched into one of her favorite hymns.

The last time she had sat in this pew and heard these same voices raised in that same music, she had been almost nineteen years old. Tucker had been away for months, and she'd been missing him desperately, loving him so much she hurt.

Love. It had started out as hero worship when he'd found her trying to stand up to a gang of bullies. He'd lit into them, busting noses and blacking eyes, scaring her half to death in the process. When she'd heard that he'd been suspended from school for a week for fighting, she'd been horrified. That was before she had discovered that suspension was nothing new for Tucker Owen. He could give lessons in toughness, in disobedience—in all the things her parents had gone to such lengths to protect her from all her life.

They might even have succeeded had it not been for a pair of steady blue-gray eyes that had stared right through her pitifully meager defenses one day and recognized them for what they were.

Miss Priss, he'd called her. Lady Goody-Good. She'd been furious with him, and she'd let him know it. She had wanted to be more like the girls she'd seen him hanging around with at school—the kind who wore miniskirts and tank tops and gaudy dangling earrings. The kind who used blue eye-shadow and smoked cigarettes, and probably other things, as well, although they were careful not to let her see them. Afraid she'd snitch, no doubt. They'd let her know more times than one that good girls were a real pain in the behind.

Tucker had been kind to her, but he'd really liked the other kind of girl. How many times had she seen him come up behind one of them in the hallway and wrap his arms around her from behind, his thumbs blatantly brushing the undersides of her breasts?

Good girls didn't allow boys to touch them that way. Oh, no. And good girls made perfect grades. They were held up in class as an example of the proper way to do everything, which made life outside the classroom sheer hell.

All the grownups said nice things about good girls, but parents didn't let them go on Halloween hayrides, because everyone knew that went on at those things.

Hope had known, too. That was why she'd wanted so desperately to be allowed to go. Gabby, the single "bad girl" who had befriended her at Princetown High, had told her all about the deliciously wicked things boys did to girls while the hay wagons plodded along Swisher's Road to the river for a wienie roast and back to town again.

Hope had gone to the Halloween parties sponsored by the church to keep children off the streets. Her parents had beamed their approval when she'd helped hand out prizes for the best costumes.

Oh, yes, approval was the reward that made up for all the things she'd wanted to do and couldn't, but she'd managed a few small rebellions, even so. For instance, she'd learned to put on a layer of pale lipstick after she'd got to school, not before, and she'd learned how to roll her waistband over to shorten her skirt. A few times she'd taken off her socks because Gabby had told her it would make her legs look sexier, but she'd ended up with blistered heels, and that had been the end of that.

Tucker had been completely outside her experience. She'd known from the very first, even when she'd been too young to understand why, that her parents would never approve of a single thing about him, from the tight jeans that emphasized his masculinity, to his shaggy hair, to the cigarettes he was seldom without, even on the school grounds.

He didn't drink, even though most of the other boys bragged about how much beer they could put away. That was something in his favor. Of course, she soon learned why. Gin-Jim. The other boys had taunted him about his father until Hope had wanted to jump on them, screaming to make them leave him alone.

That had been about the third time he had come to her rescue. About the time he'd taken to watching her unobtrusively to see that she got home safely from school. He never would go home with her to meet her parents, and gradually she came to understand that he had no interest in meeting her father.

Goodness knows she had no interest in meeting his!

One day right at break time, Gin-Jim Owen had come to school drunk as a lord to demand that his boy be allowed to quarterback for the Princetown Tigers. Hope had been in the hallway, and she'd seen it all. She could still remember the awful ache she'd felt at the sight of Tucker's face when he'd come in through a side door, blowing out a stream of smoke, and had seen his father.

The principal had threatened to call the law, and Tucker had muttered an apology. He'd said something about his father being sick, although no one had believed him. There'd been snickers and jeers as Tucker had half carried his father outside and shoved him into the truck and driven off with him.

No one had offered to help, but neither had anyone tried to stop him, in spite of the fact that Tucker had been too young for a driver's license. He'd been driving since he was twelve. Everyone understood that someone had to haul Gin-Jim home from Greasy's Tavern when he'd had too much to drink even to find the truck, much less to drive it.

And now and then he would take the old rattletrap out on the Old Mill Road and let it out to test whatever changes he'd made to the engine. That, too, they had understood.

Boys will be boys. Everybody said that, with a knowing little smile. Had anyone ever said girls will be girls?

If they had, Hope hadn't heard it.

Now she clasped her white-gloved hands in her lap as the sermon droned on. Her father was definitely the better speaker. Poor Dr. Saunders—as saintly as he might be, he'd succeeded only in putting half his audience to sleep.

It had been Hope's father who had arranged her first date with Hugh Phillips, who had lived next door to the parsonage back then. At first she'd disliked him intensely. He was a tattletale and hated to get dirty. But gradually, she'd come to see that they had a lot in common. Hugh's father, a self-made lumber tycoon who gave hoards of money to the church and had his name on all sorts of plaques attesting to his civic generosity, was determined that Hugh was going to have all the advantages that he himself had missed out on.

Poor Hugh. He had been nice looking in a translucent sort of way. His manners flawless, his grades perfect, he'd been just the sort to appeal to her parents. She'd wanted to think it was his "niceness." Occasionally, she'd wondered if it was the money.

Dr. Saunders showed signs of winding down, and Hope reached for her hymnal. It had been a good idea, coming to church. For too long, she hadn't allowed herself even to think about Hugh, about those awful four years—about the resentment that had grown in her until she almost hated him.

There were dozens of people to greet outside the church. It took almost half an hour to get through them, and in that time, Hope declined several sincere offers to "come go home to dinner." She wasn't quite ready yet to jump back into the social stream. There were bound to be questions— she could feel them now, throbbing just under the surface. Why had the Phillipses moved away so suddenly? How long had they been engaged, and why hadn't her parents announced it? What about poor Hugh's accident; was it just awful? How had he died?

What would they have said if she'd stood up during the announcements and said that the reason Daisy and Bob Ed Phillips left town so suddenly was because Hugh was caught cheating and kicked out of his prep school, in spite of the fact that his father had donated a science building—that his father had threatened to disown him, and it was all poor Daisy could do to hold her family together. Her engagement? She'd never been engaged to Hugh because she'd been in love with Tucker Owen all her life, and yes, the accident had been just awful. She would never have married him if it hadn't been for the accident, and although the doctors had given him only a few days to live, he had surprised them and lingered on for four years.

And by the time he'd died, she had almost hated him because she couldn't love him. He hadn't loved her, either. That had been Bob Ed's tragically unrealistic fantasy—that somehow, magically, they would produce a son, and the Phillips name would go on forever....

The sound of a siren came faintly from across the river. Fire, ambulance or police, she could never tell the difference. They all gave her cold chills.

"Why, Hope Outlaw, as I live and breathe! I heard you were back in town. How're your folks? I certainly do miss your father's sermons."

Before she could make her escape, Hope found herself trapped against a row of crepe myrtles by her old high school English teacher. "Thank you, Mrs. Chainey. I'll be sure and tell Daddy the next time I write. They hated to leave here, but they really enjoyed the mountains. Right now they're spending most of their time on an overseas project. They might come back for a visit when they get back to the States this fall."

"Well, you haven't changed one bit since you used to write those lovely papers for me. I always thought you'd grow up to be a writer, but— Oh, and I heard poor Hugh died. I'm so sorry—so young... I never did teach him, but he seemed like such a nice boy."

"Thank you, Mrs. Chainey," she murmured, edging away.

"You ought to try and write about it, Hope. They say it helps, and who knows—maybe it would be the start of something."

"Oh, I doubt that—I hardly even write letters any more." She reached the end of the row of shrubs next to the parking lot.

"Shame to see good talent go to waste. Well, you're still young yet... Why don't you come go home with me? We've got stewed chicken with pie bread dumplings for dinner."

Hope made her excuses and hurried toward her car. She had had enough of people for awhile. Right now all she wanted was to get away somewhere quiet, all by herself. It occurred to her that for the first time in her life, there was no reason why she couldn't do exactly that. At least until her new job began, her time was her own. She could skip church if she wanted to, spend the entire day in bed with a book, or stay up all night and eat cold pizza for breakfast. There was no one to disapprove.

And right now, what she wanted to do more than anything else was not eat chicken and dumplings and parry a lot of personal questions, but go down to the river, to a place she hadn't seen in more than seven years.

Tucker washed up the breakfast dishes and tried not to show his impatience while Billy dried and put away. "Hey, don't throw it in the cabinet! You break that plate, it'll come out of your hide!"

"I didn't ask for no handouts."

"Don't worry, you're not getting any. When you're done with the dishes, grab a broom and sweep the front porch, and then do all the way out to the end of the walk, okay?"

"Sweep? You're crazy, man. I don't push no broom. You want some jerk to clean up this place, get yourself a woman. I ain't doin' no woman's work." Billy flung down the towel on the floor and scowled across the yellow Formica-topped table.

"Sweeping's not woman's work. My old man pushed broom."

"Yeah, an' mine knocked off two liquor stores and a gas station—so what?"

Teeth clamped so tight his jaw ached, Tucker picked up the towel. "Look, kid, I got you one job and you blew it. You want another chance, you'll lose that smart mouth of yours real fast."

"Yeah? You gonna make me?"

Tucker flung the towel down across the table. He was tempted to throw in the towel figuratively, as well, but he gave it one more try. "I got an investment in you, boy. This is the third time I've bailed you out. You eat my food, you sleep under my roof, you're damned well going to hear what I have to say—is that clear?''

"I didn't sleep under your stinkin' old roof!"

Tucker had known that. At least he'd suspected it. He'd heard the boy go outside once he thought Tucker was asleep in his own room. He'd forcibly restrained himself from following, telling himself that if he came back, he could stay. If he didn't, then to hell with him. Tucker had done all he could do.

But just before daylight, Billy had come back, tiptoed into the spare room, and when Tucker had called him for breakfast this morning, he'd been curled up in a tight knot, clutching a hunk of sheet as if it were a stuffed toy.

The fire engines roared by, and Tucker went out onto the porch. God knows, fire was nothing new down here. Some of these places were little more than a bunch of kindling waiting to be touched off, and this summer, it had been worse than ever.

Pete Brendell owned the renovated mill houses. It had been fairly easy to convince him to spend some money on them after a tenant had fallen through a rotten floor and sued. The slumlords all lived up on the ridge, and Tucker knew the name of every one of them. Once the center was off and running, he planned to take on the rest of them until he got the whole community cleaned up.

He made a mental note to see about providing smoke alarms at cost to anyone who'd install one. At cost—hell, free. Ah, the devil, he'd probably end up paying people to use the damned things, but it would be worth it. Fire had been a big problem this year—even grass fires could spread and do real damage.

Billy sidled up, their quarrel evidently forgotten. "See where they went to?"

"Nah—somewhere out Third street. Probably just another grass fire." He gave the boy a sharp look. "Maybe some of those old tires rekindled, you reckon?"

Billy shrugged, the motion making his long arms and large hands waggle almost comically. "Where's yer broom? I gotta get outta here before Ma gets home from church. She promised to cook something today."

Once Billy had gone, the day stretched alluringly before Tucker, and he thought of all the things he could do with it. In his spare time, he'd been fooling around with differing rod ratios in an effort to unlock additional horsepower. He could play around with that some more. Or he could bake a cake. He'd kill the first guy who spread it around, but he'd turned into a pretty fine pastry cook, if he did say so himself. With all the mixes on the market, all a guy needed was an oven and a little imagination. That pineapple-peanut-butter-chocolate thing he'd baked last week had turned out real good, even if he had ended up eating it with a spoon.

Nah—it was too hot to bake. He'd do better to check out the center, see how it was coming along. He'd deliberately stayed away these past few days, knowing that Hope still hadn't given up yet.

The trouble was, she'd screwed up his perspective by showing up after all these years. Everything had been ticking over like clockwork—he had a neat, comfortable home in a nice neighborhood—well, maybe not so nice yet, but he was working on it. He had his work and a few good friends—what more did a guy need?

And then she'd had to show up and louse it all up for him.

Why couldn't she have changed more? If she'd let herself go, put on a few too many pounds in the wrong places, started wearing too much makeup and fancy clothes, lording it all over everybody on account of having married Phillips Enterprises, he'd have had an easier time ignoring her.

But did she have the common decency to do that? Hell, no! Instead, she'd shown up looking like the same girl he'd once put on a pedestal and worshiped, only more beautiful. And even more vulnerable. Why couldn't he hate her for what she'd done to him—to them?

Because he couldn't. God knows, he wanted to. He had every reason to, but he just couldn't.

He'd give her a week. Two, at most. It wouldn't take long before she discovered that even cleaned up, Shacktown was still no place for a River Ridge princess. Sooner or later she'd get bored and get out, and then things would settle back to normal.

Without planning it, Tucker found himself on the road that led to the part of the river where he used to meet Hope. It was hard to reach, and only by accident, when he'd been following a deer trail, had he discovered the way down to the bank.

He left his truck in the Wildlife Access area, where there was a rough boat ramp and a small graveled parking lot. There were several other vehicles there already, Sunday afternoon being a prime fishing time. Thanks to the dry spring they'd had, none of them would make it up as far as he was going. The river shoaled at the bend, and then narrowed down so that it wasn't worth the effort to drag a boat that far.

The path had grown up, but someone—probably kids sneaking off to smoke and drink beer—had been up this way quite recently. A blackberry cane had been broken back, the leaves just now beginning to wilt.

Overhead, a hawk circled lazily. A wren cut loose with a shrill series of notes that echoed in the overhanging vines. Honeysuckle and poison ivy had been bad enough, but the kudzu had taken over the whole bank and was reaching out onto the shoals. One of these mornings, Tucker thought with comfortable amusement, River Ridge was going to wake up and discover its fancy showplaces, its churches, gingerbread castles and country clubs all smothered alive in the damned stuff. Kudzu was no respecter of status. Tucker kind of liked the stuff, personally.

The river flowed black and sluggish, like liquid tar. A few wildflowers bloomed in the shallows, and he tried to remember the names.

Hope had known. She'd known the name of all the birds and all the flowers, and even all the damned rocks that washed downriver. There was one called gneiss—she'd spelled it for him, pronouncing it "nice." And another called schist, which she'd pronounced "skissed." Naturally he'd taken the cue and kissed her, and it had been nicer and nicer until it was so nice it was damned near unbearable.

But it hadn't gone any further than that. His fault. It had almost killed him, too, because sometimes it had seemed like he'd been in a constant state of arousal since he was about fourteen years old. It had got so that when he'd park his truck and head down to the river, he'd be hard before he ever got there.

Damned if he wasn't in the same shape now, just remembering!

He should've brought along his fishing gear. Or better yet, taken the Chevy Lumina he had just finished rebuilding, out onto the track and let 'er out flat until he'd got his head straightened out.

It was this place, Tucker thought as he lay back in the familiar clearing—the greenness, the birds, the smell of honeysuckle and river mud. He'd brought Hope here about a hundred times before he'd ever so much as kissed her, because she wasn't like other girls. She was special. She didn't know the moves, and one part of him hadn't wanted to teach her, but the other part—the part of him over which he'd fought a constant battle for control—that part had wanted to unbutton her white cotton blouse and take off her pleated skirt and strip off every speck of white cotton underwear. He'd known she would wear white cotton underwear long before he ever saw it.

But he'd only held her and kissed her a little bit—no real deep stuff—until the summer after he'd first gone off to school. He'd been late getting started at Tech, because he'd had to earn enough money first, and even then, he'd had to go on the co-op plan, which meant working three months, going to school three months, with damned little time off for good behavior.

Or bad.

Hope had written. He doubted that her parents had known about the letters. She'd told him everything, about wanting to work at the Hut with Gabby and having to work with Miss Eula at the Kiddy Cat instead, because her parents thought it was more suitable.

Suitable, crap! It had been a dumping place for River Ridge brats while their folks played bridge, or golf, or drank their three-hour luncheons. If she'd wanted to baby-sit, he could have told her, even then, about a dozen women who were desperate to find a decent place to leave their children while they worked or looked for work.

He hadn't, of course. He hadn't written much, because he wasn't real comfortable with letters, and he was afraid his spelling wasn't very good. And when he'd been home, they'd had other things to talk about. Such as how he was going to graduate with an engineering degree and go somewhere and work his way up until he was running his own company.

And how she was going to own her own day-care center one of these days, where she could make the rules instead of having them made by a woman who still mourned the way the country had gone downhill since the death of Calvin Coolidge.

Neither of them had talked about a future together—not at first. He'd dreamed, though...and planned. He'd had his goals.

Hope had told him all about Hugh, and how their parents pushed them together, and how they'd gotten to be friends because they had so much in common—mostly their parents. But Hugh had never kissed her, she'd told him gravely—never even tried to.

Maybe it had started by Tucker's wanting to prove he was ten times the man Hugh Phillips would ever be. That last summer, kissing and holding and petting above the waist hadn't been enough. They had both known it with that breathless sort of awareness that cuts to the bone when you're young and in love and unsure.

He had never gone under her skirt because he'd known that once he touched her there, there would be no turning back. He would have taken her, and it would have ruined everything, because in a whole lot of ways, she'd been more child than woman, even then.

But the summer he'd taken three weeks off to get his grandmother settled in a nursing home in Wilson, he had come home afterward. Hope had been seventeen—almost eighteen, and still as squeaky clean as she'd been the first time he'd laid eyes on her. It was a quality she carried inside her, he decided.

"You know what I want to do, don't you?" he'd whispered after a kiss that had gone on until both of them were burning and breathless.

"I know. Please, Tuck—I want you to—to do it."

"Sugar love, you don't know what you're asking." Her cotton skirt had fallen back when he'd lowered her onto the bed of honeysuckle, and he'd laid his hand over her knee first, and then began to move it slowly upward until he touched the elastic leg of her underpants.

"Yes I do. Tucker, I love you. I'll never love anyone else, and I can't bear to wait any longer, because you'll go away and leave me again and when you're gone, I can't think of anything but you—and I want to have something more to remember until you come home again. Please?"

"Sweet Jesus, honey, don't say that." He'd thought about his mother then—about how her whole life had been ruined because of one stolen moment, and he'd known he couldn't risk it—not with Hope. He was prepared—it was considered the macho thing for a guy to carry protection in his billfold, but his packet was so old, it had probably self-destructed long before now.

So he'd kissed her, meaning to ease off, and before they'd realized it, she'd been lying there on the cool, crushed, greenness with her blouse and her skirt and her slip hanging on a black walnut sapling where they'd caught when he'd tossed them aside. Her skin had been so flawless, so milky white, he could only stare at what he'd uncovered. With her golden hair coming loose to spread about her head, she'd been so beautiful—so perfect—that at first he'd been afraid even to touch her.

Her breasts were small, but they'd fit the palms of his hands just fine. Lying down, they'd sort of settled onto her chest like small mounds of melting vanilla ice cream, with pale cherries on top, and he'd had to taste them—to taste the unbelievable sweetness of her.

She had curled right up in his arms with a little whimper, and he'd held her while they both struggled to draw air into their lungs. And then he'd slipped off her spotless white sneakers, her white socks, and still on his knees before her, he'd slowly removed her white cotton underpants.

They weren't anything fancy, not like others he had seen. They came all the way up to her waist and covered her hips completely, but when he peeled them down and saw the tiny dimple of her navel, he almost lost it right there.

Clutching her pants in his shaking hand, he had stared down at the wispy clutter of pale curls that revealed her shadowy cleft. A cold sweat had broken out on his back, and if lightning had struck three feet away at that moment, he would never even have looked up.

"Aren't you—that is, don't you want to—?" she'd stammered as her face and the upper part of her chest had flushed a dull red.

Want to! God, he'd been crippled from wanting. He'd wanted to love every sweet inch of her sweet body and then start all over again—and again and again—until he was an old man and she was an old woman, and neither of them could remember exactly why they were lying on a riverbank in a bed of honeysuckle, with hawks circling lazily overhead and a thundercloud threatening to dump on them any minute.

He'd been paralyzed.

"Take off yours, too," she'd pleaded softly. "I want to see you—all over."

"Oh—yeah. I mean—" His voice had sounded as if he were trying out for the boy's choir, so he'd shut up.

And then he'd tried to explain. About not wanting to hurt her, and wanting her first time to be perfect, and not wanting to take a chance on ruining her life.... He remembered talking a lot and sweating a lot, and trying to hide his arousal from her.

She'd misunderstood. Thinking he was disappointed in her, she'd gotten her feelings hurt, and naturally he'd had to comfort her, and it had started all over again.

God, what a day. He'd loved her in all the ways a man can love a woman, but one. She'd been reluctant at first—embarrassed. But then she'd started panting, and she'd shuddered while he held her and caressed her, and the next thing he knew, damned if they both hadn't been crying!

Of course, he'd never let her see his tears.

Now, a hundred years later, Tucker rolled over onto his stomach and buried his face in his arms. He felt as if he'd been reamed out until there was nothing left but a hollow, brittle shell.

After awhile, he slept.

When he opened his eyes again, his face still buried in his arms, he wondered what had alerted him. A crow? A drop of rain? A fisherman around the bend, cursing or bragging too loudly?

And then it came again—the swishing sound of someone moving through the bushes. He sat up, rubbed his eyes and glanced at the sky. It was time to leave, anyhow. He'd wasted half the day, but at least he'd gotten a pretty decent nap out of it.

He was on his feet, looking for the moccasins he'd kicked off earlier, when she stepped into the clearing. For a minute he thought he had dredged her up out of his imagination.

But then she spoke. "Tucker? I thought I recognized your truck down by the boat ramp. I saw a few boats out on the river—I thought maybe you were fishing or something."

"Nah—just relaxing, trying to get rid of a headache." He'd been working up to a headache all day. This was just what he needed to bring it out in full force. He took in everything about her in one narrowed, seemingly careless glance. She was wearing an orange shirt with a white cotton skirt and white sandals. No white sneakers and rolltop socks this time, but he'd be willing to bet she was wearing white underwear. Cotton.

With a deliberate effort, Tucker hardened himself against the memories. She had made her feelings clear enough when she'd gone to Boston to marry Phillips without even having the decency to get in touch with him first. He'd had to hear it from one of the guys at the garage. Naturally, he'd gone directly to her parents, and her mother had confirmed it, telling him that Hope and Hugh had a lovely apartment in Boston and were planning to stay there indefinitely.

With a smile that never came near his eyes, he said, "Welcome to the coolest spot in town, princess. Happens I'm just leaving, so you can have it all to yourself."

Five

___

He might just as well have hit her. Even from a dozen feet away, Tucker could see the hurt in her eyes. "Yeah, well... nice day for it, anyway. I just came down here to uh—cool off."

That, at least, should not be too hard to believe, the way he was sweating.

Thunder rumbled softly in the background, and the small patch of sky visible above the treetops was streaked like a dark gray tabby cat. Not a leaf stirred. Tucker wished he had never given in to the impulse to come here today. Or ever. In fact, he wished to hell he had never followed a certain moving van to a certain tall, turreted Victorian house on River Ridge Road one afternoon some seventeen or so years ago.

"I hope you're not angry about the murals," Hope said rather tentatively. "I just thought it might brighten the rooms up some."

Murals? *"Rooms?"*

"Three since the partitions went up, but I left Gabby's walls the way they were. They're just in the playroom and the Land of Nod."

Tucker hitched up his jeans by the belt loops. They rode low on his long waist because that was the way he was built, but lately, they seemed to ride lower than ever. It was too damned hot to eat, was the trouble.

"The land of *what*?" he said.

Hope shifted her weight to the other foot, and his gaze followed every nuance of movement. "Of nod?" she whispered. It was more a question than a statement.

"What the f—what the hell—" He cleared his throat and started over again, conscious of a pounding in his head that had nothing at all to do with astigmatism. "And what, pray tell, is a nod?"

She shifted her weight once more, and Tucker wished devoutly that she'd kept her sweet body in one place. "The land of... You know, the Land of Nod? Little babies? Sleeping?"

"Is this code of yours supposed to have some profound relevance?"

With a look of exasperation, Hope tilted her head to one side. "Oh, for goodness' sake, didn't your mother ever read you any nursery rhymes?"

"No, but my pa was a pretty good hand. His favorite was 'Sing a song of sixpence,' pockets full of rye. Or bourbon. But mostly gin."

She closed her eyes without speaking, and again, Tucker felt like a man who'd just kicked a stray mutt in the rump. Worse. She hadn't even growled at him. "So look," he said in a conscious effort to assuage his conscience, "What about those partitions? I've been kind of busy this past week—I've got three carburetors and a modified mechanical fuel pump headed down to Daytona next week, and two of my best men are out sick. At least one's sick—the other's on his honeymoon. Same difference."

Without another word, Hope wandered over to the place where he had crushed a bed in the honeysuckle earlier. She sat down, drawing her knees up and covering her legs with her skirt. And then she plucked a pale yellow blossom and carefully sucked the nectar from the hollow tube.

Tucker waited. And watched. A shaft of pale sunlight set fire to the tendrils that danced on the surface of her sleek hairstyle. Its baby fine texture would always defeat her best efforts. How well he remembered teasing her about . . .

Clearing his throat, he scowled. "So what about it? Those partitions do all right for you? I told the contractor to do whatever Gabby told him to. And the plumber—was he able to fix you up with a set of sawed-off fixtures?"

Hope closed her eyes. She'd been doing a lot of that just lately. As if by not looking at something, she could make it go away. "It's all perfect. Thank you. The washrooms have to be scaled down for the littlest ones."

With seeming casualness, Tucker settled onto the ground some ten feet away. "These murals you mentioned—what kind of stuff are we talking about?"

"Nothing like what you're afraid of." She smiled and quickly averted her face, but not quickly enough. He'd seen it.

Tucker edged closer, levering himself along in a seated position with his hands and feet. "Oh yeah?" he growled. He'd give her a month. By then she would have had her fill of Shacktown. She could bow out with a clear conscience, knowing she'd done her bit for the less fortunate.

"When I got in touch with the kids the high school art teacher had recommended, they were all afraid to do anything. They said the word was out—Tucker Owen would chop off the first hand that lifted a spray-paint can to one of his walls."

Reluctantly, Tucker began to chuckle. Without knowing how it came about, he was talking to her about paint and politics, and she was talking about plumbing and partitions, and then Tucker found himself telling her all about butting heads with the established business community across the river, and how he'd finally moved them off dead center by buying the old plug tobacco factory and donating it to the city.

"Once I'd done that, they had to cough up. See, they never expected me to pull it off, but I had help they hadn't counted on. Some of the NASCAAR drivers owed me a favor. They kind of liked what I was trying to do, especially since Buck Earnhardt is a favorite on the circuit. You knew he grew up two streets over from the old ruin, didn't you? Place used to be a hangout for winos. Oh, the structure was good for another hundred years, but the inside was a real mess. Anyhow, Buck—"

At Hope's puzzled look, he said, "You never heard of B. K. Earnhardt? He's been qualifying in the low eight all season. Won the pole at the Winston Invitational last year at Rockingham, but he blew a tire going into the last lap."

"I'm afraid I've never followed automobile racing." She looked at him warily, and Tuck ceased his sideways movement. He'd thought he was being subtle about it. Hell, he only wanted to get close enough so they didn't have to yell over half an acre of weeds.

"Yeah, well...I don't spend too much time at the speedways these days, either. Mostly I just send parts." Thunder drowned out the words. "Anyhow, ol' Buck raised a bunch of money for us, and he's going to be at the grand opening, along with a few more of the guys."

Hope murmured something polite and ambiguous, and then neither of them could think of anything else to say. She stared at a blue jay that had landed in the top of a young black walnut tree, and Tucker stared at her.

"So," he said finally. "Got any idea how many kids you're going to be taking in?"

"Gabby says eleven women have signed up so far, and most of them have more than one child."

"Maybe I should've turned over more of the building to you girls."

She gave him a wry look. "No one's called me a girl in a long time, Tucker."

"Aw, hell—don't tell me that living up north has turned you into one of those female snapping turtles. I opened a door for a lady at the hardware store last week, and she like to've taken my head off. You'd think I'd goosed her or something."

Again Hope tried to hide her smile from him.

"O' course, if you want to call me boy, that's all right with me. My grandma called me boy until I was nearly twenty-five years old, but since she also talked about her 'girlfriends,' not a one of 'em under eighty, I didn't have the heart to fuss with her about it."

This time they laughed together, and Tucker felt something inside him begin to unfold and reach out.

"I didn't even know you had a grandmother," she said, and then, "But yes, I do remember something a long time ago—you said she was the one who made you promise not to drop out of school, and since she scared the bejabbers out of you, you didn't dare let her down."

"Yeah, that's Miz Emma, all right. Used to live down near Southport."

"Is she still—?"

"Nah, she died last year. She was in a nursing home in Wilson for a few years before that, and she didn't know me anymore—which was just as well, I reckon, seeing's how nothing I ever did was good enough to suit her."

As a matter of fact, that had been the reason he had dropped out of engineering school just short of getting his degree. He'd no longer been able to manage both tuition and nursing home expenses, and at that time, he'd had no royalties coming in from his patents.

"I'm sorry," Hope said, and she gave a funny little shrug as if she knew the words were inadequate, but what else could she say?

"It happens." He shrugged, too. They were both finding it increasingly hard to avoid the personal.

And then he deliberately blew it. "So, how did marriage suit you? Your mama said you had a real nice place up in Boston."

"You talked to Mama?"

"I, uh—just happened to run into her one day." *When I marched up to your front door and damned near took it off the hinges.* "I asked how you were getting on and all." *If you believe that's what I asked her, you're crazier than I am.* "No big deal."

Thunder was rumbling in earnest now, and from a distance, Tucker could hear the sound of pickups being started, backing down to the ramp to haul out fishing boats. He felt like a first-class jerk, and because he was embarrassed, he made things worse. "So, what was it like? I reckon you had it real nice up there, didn't you? Maids, butlers—the works. What's Boston's version of River Ridge like, anyway? I never got around to going up to see the Constitution. Always meant to, but somehow, I never made it."

He couldn't seem to shut up. Before he even finished talking, he knew he'd blundered into something way out of his depth, and the fact that he'd deliberately tried to hurt her made it worse.

He was shaping an apology when she spoke. "It was—all right, I guess. About what I expected. And yes, I was fortunate enough to have plenty of help."

She began rearranging her skirt, and he knew she was going to leave him. He didn't blame her. In her place, he would've kicked his tail halfway across the river, but then, Hope was a lady.

Oh, hell.

It was like the time he'd had a real bad toothache. He hadn't been able to let it alone, worrying it with his tongue, even though the slightest pressure near about killed him. *Say you're sorry, you jackass! The woman lost her husband— the least you can do is say you're sorry!*

"Looks like we might be going to get some rain after all," he said instead. "Been dry enough. Brushfires almost every day, seems like."

"I heard the sirens." Hope rose and brushed off her skirt. "Uh-oh, grass stains," she murmured, and without looking directly at him, she turned toward the narrow footpath.

Tucker fell in behind her. Neither of them spoke during the short walk through the woods, and after the first couple of minutes, he had sense enough not to watch her backside swaying so beguilingly as she ducked under swags of kudzu and sidestepped huckleberry bushes that never bore anything larger than a seed-tick.

It was sprinkling by the time they reached the Wildlife Access area. He'd driven one of the shop's blue-and-silver pickups with Owen Automotive on the side, and parked it all the way over on the left-hand side. Her red compact—not at all the kind of car he would have expected her to be driving—was all the way over to the other side. They were the only two vehicles left in the parking lot.

"Well...see you around," Hope said, standing in her open door.

Looking at her, all Tucker could think about was a time when he'd been about five and had made himself a toy boat out of a shingle and a stick. He'd taken it down to the river and launched it, fully convinced that it would do his bidding, because he was the captain. He'd watched it get caught up in the current and sail away. Nearly out of sight, he'd seen it hit a snag and go under, and then he'd lost sight of it completely.

He hadn't cried. He'd told himself it wasn't a real boat, anyhow. Who cared about an old chunk of wood?

"Yeah," he said gruffly. "See you around."

The day of the grand opening drew near, and preparations took on a note of hysteria. The center was constantly overrun with people, all intent on their own projects. Men with tool belts clanked up and down the hallways, dodging

Shacktown women who were dragging in refurbished furniture and prize potted plants, and River Ridge club women intent on seeing that their donations had been properly used, and that the plaque bearing the name of their organization was given a suitably prominent position.

Teenagers, some of whom were helping out, some of whom were there out of curiosity, seemed to be everywhere. Billy Coe had turned out to be an enormous help. Hope was delighted that she hadn't once had to remind him not to ride his skateboard inside the building. She'd even seen him chase out a few others who had dared try.

He was standing on the ladder, hanging colorful flags that had been sewn for them by a neighborhood seamstress, when Elsie Brendell stopped by early one morning.

"Hope, I missed you at church last Sunday. You got away before I could speak to you."

"Oh—Mrs. Brendell. It's nice to see you again. Have you met Billy Coe? Billy, this is Mrs. Brendell. Her group donated that lovely furniture in the lobby."

Billy blushed, Elsie Brendell lifted a pair of impeccably pencilled brows, and ignoring the boy, went on to say, "I know this is short notice, but I'm having a small group of people in for dinner tonight, and we're counting on your being there, dear."

Hope immediately began lining up excuses like a row of tin soldiers, but before she could deploy a single one, the older woman rushed on to say, "It will be just a few of your parents' old friends, and we're all dying to hear how they liked Weaverville, and how Bob Ed Phillips is getting along. We were all so shocked to hear about poor Daisy, and right on top of that, poor Hugh—!"

Dark eyes snapping, Hope said, "Mrs. Brendell, I'm—"

"Oh, call me Elsie, dear—after all, there's not all that much difference in our ages these days, is there?"

There was at least two decades, unless she'd had cosmetic surgery done on her birth certificate, as well as her face, but Hope was far too well brought up to mention such a possibility. "I'm afraid I'll be to busy getting ready for the opening, Mrs. Brendell—Elsie. You wouldn't believe how many last-minute details there are. But thank you for asking me."

The svelte, auburn-haired woman laid a hand on her arm and leaned forward in a wave of Chanel. "But, darling, we all have to eat. And your sweet mama would never forgive me if I neglected her little girl, so—"

"—all these thank-you notes to write to the people who donated toys, and—"

"—about seven? We're dining out on the patio, and afterward, there's croquet—Peter's installed new garden lights, and my magnolias are magnificent this year. Or maybe you'd rather—"

"—and my car hasn't been starting all that regularly, so I don't like to venture out after—"

"—your bathing suit, because I'm sure the guests will be in and out of the pool. Remember when you were a little girl, and—"

"Mrs. Brendell—"

"Hush now, honey, not another word. You've been working so hard on all this . . ." She gestured vaguely at the clutter of tables, cribs and pint-size chairs, some of them still not uncrated. "I'd never forgive myself is we let you wear yourself out before you even get settled in again. We'll look for you about seven, all right?" And then, hardly pausing for breath—"Oh, Agnes, you're just the one I've been looking for!"

Hope nodded weakly as the woman hurried away to join her friend. It had been bound to happen sooner or later, she told herself. Perhaps it would be better to get it over with, so she could begin to relax.

"Man, if that old broad ever comes gunnin' for me, I'm outta here!" Billy placed his nail and hung the last pennant, an orange-and-pink one depicting a flat, appliquéd Humpty-Dumpty. "Can I help you unpack all this junk, Miss Hope?"

Together, they uncrated the rest of the furniture and placed it roughly in position. It would be fine-tuned later, after she gave the place a thorough final cleaning.

Gabby emerged from her office, where she'd been arranging stacks of largely empty files in her secondhand, repainted filing cabinet. "Anybody hungry?"

Billy looked up hopefully and then ducked his head again. "I already ate," he mumbled. He had been waiting when Hope and Gabby arrived just before nine, and he'd worked steadily ever since. Gabby was beginning to tease Hope about her young conquest—which, of course, was ridiculous—but never in Billy's hearing.

"Burgers? Salad bar?" Gabby perched on a child-size table and propped her espadrilles—green ones today—on the back of a chair.

"What I'd really like is a bowl of Lin Tuan's chili," Hope said, praying her stomach wouldn't turn on her. She'd never been in the place in her life, but she'd heard it was cheap, adequate, and best of all, there was no dress code. Pants or skirts were required; the rest was optional. Besides, Lin Tuan, like most of the other nearby merchants, had donated toward furnishing the community center.

Hope glanced at Billy, who was shoeless and shirtless, his jeans filthy enough to stand alone. "Billy—go with us? You don't have to eat again if you don't want to, but I'm not really comfortable in a place like that without a male escort."

The chili was delicious. Billy reluctantly agreed to let himself accept a bowl of chili as partial compensation for all the work he'd put in on their behalf. As for Gabby, she ordered a triple-burger, fries and a shake, and then sat back to enjoy the scenery, which consisted primarily of construction workers, linesmen, a street-marking crew and a couple of patrolmen sitting beside the open front window where they could monitor their car radios.

Hope made herself as inconspicuous as possible and tried to ignore the looks and remarks aimed at their booth. Billy inhaled the first bowl of chili and accepted a refill, while Gabby leaned back and frankly enjoyed the ambience.

By six-thirty that evening, Hope had worried herself into a splitting headache and was wishing laryngitis would strike so she'd have an excuse not to go—or at least not to talk, if she went.

What could she tell them? The truth?

What *was* the truth? To this day she hadn't figured out how she could have gone to visit a critically injured friend at her parents' insistence, and ended up married to him.

"Poor Hugh needs you," her mother had said. "You two have always been so close." They hadn't. Not really. "We've all looked forward to sharing our grandchildren, and now..."

Hope had never been able to deny her mother, and when her mother cried, why then, there was no way she could not have gone to Boston. Could her parents have known about her feelings for Tucker? Was that why they had pushed her into a marriage with no hope of a future? Just to get her away from Princetown until her father got his new church?

Her mother had always impressed on Hope the fact that she came from a "good" family. From the time she'd been old enough to drop her own coin in the collection plate, she'd been encouraged to be kind to those less fortunate.

But when it came to getting personally involved with one of those "less fortunate" ones, she'd been told in no uncertain terms that they were "not our kind of people."

Hope had never considered Tucker less fortunate. She knew about his family, of course—everyone did. And that he'd always had to work for everything he got, unlike Hugh, who received an enormous allowance. Still, she'd always considered Tucker the only truly free person she knew, and she'd envied him that freedom from the bottom of her heart. No one *expected* anything of him. He didn't always have to be thinking first of what someone else would say. He could go where he wanted to, when he wanted to, and with whom. He could do more or less anything he wanted to do, and there was no one to shame him by telling him they'd expected better of him.

Hugh. Poor Hugh; he'd been just as hemmed in as she was by parental expectations. They used to compare notes and talk about what they would do once they were living on their own.

It was after spending a week at the Phillipses' summer place at Roaring Gap that her mother had first speculated on how nice it would be when Hugh and Hope married and had children. Hope had been fifteen and head over heels in love with Tucker, and scared to death someone would discover why she liked to ride her bike down by the river on hot summer afternoons.

She'd said something about not being in love with Hugh, and her mother had assured her that love would come naturally once they were married. Good Lord, what an antidiluvian notion!

It hadn't. Not really. "Oh, Hugh, I'm sorry, but I just don't know what to tell them if they ask," she whispered to the reflection in the steamy bathroom mirror.

Perhaps she had loved him as a friend—at first, at least, before pain had made him so hateful, making her feel so trapped. If he'd been her brother—or even her sister—she would have loved him. He'd been fond of her, too, but only that. He'd always seemed to prefer the company of his roommate from school—the one who had come to visit that time after he'd been kicked out for cheating.

Hope sighed and brushed a damp hand over her hair, as if it would stay smooth any longer than it took it to dry out. She would tell them exactly what she'd told Gabby—no more, no less. It was the truth, as far as it went.

Tucker knew he couldn't avoid her forever. His work was suffering, his temper was suffering, and his conscience felt like a pair of new shoes that were two sizes too small.

He had avoided the center for the past two days, but dammit, with the place getting ready to open, he couldn't stay away any longer! If she was ticked off at him, then that was just too bad. He'd told her she had no business horning in on his side of the river. If she couldn't take a few mild remarks from him, she might as well hang it up right now. Because she was going to hear a hell of a lot worse, if she hadn't already.

Okay, so he'd been a little out of line. He didn't have the benefit of a River Ridge background, or any la-de-da prep school.

Which was no excuse at all for the way he'd pushed, he admitted to himself. One thing about a college education— when you loused up, you were smart enough to know it.

And he'd loused up, royally. There'd been a time when Tucker had felt good just being around Hope Outlaw. Just thinking about her. It had been about the only time he felt good about himself—really strong and in control. She'd done that for him. He'd always felt like somebody special when he was with her, and he'd liked feeling that way.

But hell, nothing lasts forever.

Once in a blue moon, he'd told her that day when they'd nearly gone over the edge, a guy gets lucky and finds the perfect woman. Someone so pure, so sweet, so wonderful, that she makes him feel like he has to be twice as good, twice as smart just to deserve her—and twice as big and tough just so he can take care of her.

Well, he wasn't twice as old, yet, but he was getting there. And if he was big or tough, it sure as shooting wasn't on account of any holier-than-thou little preacher's girl.

First he went to the community center. She wasn't there, but he deliberately took his time looking the place over. Somehow, the pride and satisfaction he usually felt wasn't enough for him today.

Without planning it, he found himself on the road that led to Gabby's apartment. She had mentioned that Hope was still staying with her, and he figured it was only until she could find herself a fancy place on the other side of the river—if not on the ridge, at least within spitting distance.

Hope's car was in the parking lot beside the behemoth that Gabby drove, and Tucker pulled into the one remaining space and started rehearsing what he was going to say.

You don't belong on my side of the river, dammit—stay out of my territory and leave me in peace!

He couldn't say that to her. He might think it, and she might know he was thinking it, but he knew he was going to stick to something a lot safer. Like, "Haven't seen you around much lately. How's it been going?"

The trick was to sneak up on her and catch her off guard. She'd probably say something polite about the weather, and then he could say the place was looking real fine, and she'd been doing a swell job, and then he could sort of ease into telling her about this other woman he had in mind for the position, who needed the work real bad.

Yeah, that was the way to play it.

"Tucker?"

He jerked around, slammed the side of his hand against the steering wheel, and swallowed a curse as he looked out to see Gabby Boger standing beside his car.

"I wasn't sure it was you. You waiting for somebody?"

"Nah, I was just—ah..."

"Then come on in and have a glass of iced coffee with me. Lordy, if it doesn't rain pretty soon, we're going to be in a real mess. Daddy says his fields are so dried up he can sit out on the front porch swing and hear the ground cracking right wide open. Those few sprinkles we had last Sunday didn't even lay the dust."

He followed her because he felt a little foolish to have been caught hanging around outside. He was too embarrassed to say he'd been working up his nerve to go in and see Hope, and embarrassment always made him feel like going out and picking a fight with the biggest bastard he could find.

He thought he'd outgrown that stage.

"You wanting to see Hope?"

He trudged up to the second floor, following her swishing skirt and her powerful perfume. So much for salvaging his pride. "Yeah," he grunted, "Just happened to be passing by... thought I'd stop in and say hello."

"Tough, you just missed her. She's gone out to dinner, but come on in anyway, I've got some stuff to go over with you."

"I saw her car..." *Of course her car's still here, you jerk—a woman doesn't drive herself out on a date!*

"Oh, that old clunker. I think she needs a new battery, but Hope's trying to hold out until we get our first paycheck."

Torn between wanting to ask who she'd gone out with, and what the devil she'd done with all the money she'd married, Tucker said nothing. He followed Gabby inside the apartment and looked around, as if hoping she would somehow be there, after all.

"Why don't I go fix us some iced coffee, and then you can steer me through a few miles of red tape. I thought running a restaurant was bad, but it was a snap compared to this day-care thing. The government has you so hog-tied you can't even sneeze without filling out another blessed form!"

She had exaggerated the red tape, Tucker decided some time later. Either that or she'd pretty much handled it herself. He answered a few questions about what had to go through the committee and what didn't, drank two glasses of iced coffee, and then made his excuses. It was pushing ten o'clock already, and if by some chance Hope got back from her date early, he damned well didn't want to be caught hanging around her doorstep like a lovesick tomcat!

"Sure you don't want to wait for Hope? She'll probably be back pretty soon."

"Nah, I was just passing by anyway. I'd better shove off, but thanks for the refreshment. It hit the spot." Actually, he was considerably relieved that the woman who would be handling the business end of the day-care facility wasn't quite the lush he'd feared.

He was just about to back out of his space when a late model Jaguar swung into the parking lot. The driver stopped in the middle, blocking him off completely, and Tucker waited impatiently for him to discharge his freight and move on. Be a damned shame to put a dent in about thirty thousand dollars' worth of hardware.

Watching through the rearview mirror, he determined that the dude was no local. The luxury car bore a Virginia plate— a personalized one. "JQM3," he read aloud. Sighing, he switched off the ignition and watched as JQM3 got out and went around to the passenger side, and then he felt his gut tighten up like he'd swallowed a bucket of concrete.

Hope was wearing something pale and filmy, and the light was shining through her hair, making it look as if she had a halo. The smooth dude in the white jacket had handed her out of the car as if she were made of spun sugar or something. Still holding her hand, he began to move his lips.

She shook her head.

Tucker would've given three patents and his left arm to hear what was being said.

JQM3 said something else, and again, Hope shook her head, but the smile she gave him tore a strip off Tucker's hide and left him hurting right down to his naked soul.

He dropped his gaze from the mirror and waited for the Jag to move off. Then, without even looking to see if she'd gone inside, he burned about ten bucks' worth of rubber off his radials getting out of there.

Six

The day of the opening dawned still and hot. By nine o'clock in the morning there were tall, gray-centered thunderheads building up on the horizon. Tucker was on the scene early. The pig-picking crew had been there all night, as had Billy Coe.

"Had any breakfast, son?" Tucker asked, sauntering across the graveled area that had been chosen for the enormous portable grill.

Billy, wearing ragged jeans and a black death's head T-shirt, sat hunched over on an upturned ten-gallon bucket. "Sure, I had me some breakfast," he muttered.

"Then come keep me company while I have mine. Some things I want to go over with you—I can't be everywhere today, and I'm going to need all the help I can round up."

With seeming reluctance, Billy let himself be talked into accompanying Tucker to Lin Tuan's, where—also with seeming reluctance—he allowed himself to be talked into tucking into a breakfast of fried ham, fried tomatoes, biscuits and gravy.

"You been out there all night?" Tucker asked.

Billy shrugged.

"Heard you helped tend the fire. I appreciate it, boy, but you gotta go home sometime. Your ma'll be worried about you."

"She knows I can take care of myself. Better'n she can, too."

Without seeming to, Tucker studied the sullen expression on the old-young face. The last thing he needed in his life right now was a tough punk out to make trouble for himself. He should have known the first time he'd gone to bat for the kid, when he'd been hauled in for slashing tires and breaking a few windshields, that he was taking on more problems than he could skillfully juggle.

But the kid had problems, too, and at fourteen, some of them could look pretty insurmountable. Not that slashing the tires and bashing the windshields on the cars that had been parked in front of his mother's house all night was going to solve anything. Still, Tucker had understood the impotent rage that had led him to strike out at the nearest target. Wanda Coe had been a small-time hooker before she'd married. She'd been straight ever since until her husband had been sent up—a good neighbor and a good mother. Since then—well, the neighbors had been tolerant. A woman had to make a living, and unfortunately, Wanda had only one kind of job training.

"Okay, Billy, if you've got the time, here's what I need you to take care of for me today."

Some ten minutes later, Billy polished off the last of Tucker's toast and palmed the remaining jelly container and half a dozen sugar packets. "Lemme see if I got this straight— You want me to rat on any o' the guys I see doing stuff they hadn't oughtta?"

"It's called security duty, Billy. You want the place to go back to being a firetrap—another hangout for winos?"

"Brick don't burn."

"Yeah, but there's a helluva lot more in that place be-sides brick. You know what to look out for. Minimum wage for as long as you can stick it. If you're not interested, I'll get a couple of the other guys."

"Hey, did I say I wasn't interested?"

"Okay, then—just keep an eye out for anything that looks like trouble. Kids in places they shouldn't be, hassles in the parking lot—whatever. I'm going to issue you a handset so you can get in touch with me in a hurry if you need me. You feel easy with that?"

Billy shrugged his skinny shoulders. "Yeah, I'm easy. I reckon Miss Hope'll be too busy keeping up with all them brats to..."

"To what?"

"Nothing! Hey, look, if I'm gonna do all this stuff, we gotta get going."

"Things aren't supposed to get underway until eleven."

"Huh! That's all you know."

By the time they got back, the playground was swarm-ing, bystanders were three deep around the barbecue pit, and the thunderheads had moved in until they practically met overhead.

Tucker swore, and then broke off to greet the woman who had lived three doors down from him all his life. "Nice to see you, Miss Polly."

"They tell me I can get my blood pressure in this here center house of yours, Tucker."

"That's a fact, Miss Polly. Every Thursday there'll be a nurse here to take your blood pressure and talk to you about any special problems you've got."

"Well, there's my kitchen...it's sunk so low now that ever' time it rains, the water comes in right under the back door."

"Yes'm, Miss Polly. Don't you worry about that today, though. You just go on over under those trees where we've set up those chairs, and—"

"They're setting up a tent. You fixing to have a gospel meeting, Tucker?"

With a harried look at the sky, Tucker took the old woman's arm and led her over to where several other women had gathered to watch the proceedings. "No, ma'am, but we're going to have some real good music, so if you don't feel like dancing, promise me you'll do some serious clapping and stomping, all right?"

The tent had been ordered on stand-by, and it looked as if they were going to need it. It also looked as if they were going to have to open up the entire building for more than just the planned walk-through inspection tour—which meant rounding up at least a dozen more volunteers to police traffic. After today, he didn't anticipate much of a problem with security, but with this crowd...

And it wasn't even ten o'clock yet.

He saw her the minute she arrived. Gabby was driving. Evidently, Hope's car was still out of commission. Tucker made a mental note to check it out before the day was over, and another one to send a contractor who owed him a favor over to Miss Polly's house to do some ditching and inspecting for termites, leaks and anything else repairable.

Hope was wearing a denim skirt with a yellow shirt. There was nothing at all sexy about the outfit, yet all he could see was the gentle swell of her bosom and those long, sweetly curved legs.

Without meaning to, he stopped on his way from the sound truck to the podium and watched her as she slipped inside the play yard. Halfway there she turned and looked straight at him, and he felt his heart slam into the wall of his chest and flip over.

You still belong to me, girl. You could never belong to any other man. Deny it, and we'll both know you're lying!

"Miss Hope?"

Hope stared across the playground at the tall, magnificent man in moccasins, chinos and a blue chambray shirt. The cool white sunlight highlighted his dark hair and his deeply tanned face, giving him a strangely metallic look.

She shivered in spite of the humid heat.

"Miss Hope?" The voice tugged at her with the persistence of a mosquito. Oblivious, she went on staring at Tucker.

What on earth had she been thinking of when she'd agreed to come back home? Had she honestly thought he would be gone? Or that they could pick up the pieces as if her marriage had never happened? Or that they could both live in the same town without remembering? Without wanting more than a casual friendship?

Perhaps it was just that easy for him, but for her, it grew more impossible with each passing day. One part of her wanted to run to him and bury herself in his arms, to feel safe and protected and loved once again. Fortunately, the other part had better sense.

Too much had changed. She was no longer a girl, yet he insisted on seeing her as some sort of china doll that would be broken if it was taken down off the shelf and handled too roughly—that is, when he wasn't actively despising her.

"Miss Hope, you okay?"

"What—? Oh, Billy—I didn't see you there."

Surrounded by dozens of rambunctious children and swarms of people drawn by the smell of barbecuing meat and the tuning up an assortment of stringed instruments, she had seen only one man.

"Hey, listen—you want me to get them young'uns inside for you? Them clouds is gonna bust right wide open in a minute."

"Oh—yes, we'd better do that, hadn't we? I'm supposed to have three volunteers for today. If you see Debbie or Reba or Jenny, tell them I could really use a hand, will you?"

Despite the rain, the celebration was a huge success. The NASCAAR celebrities, including Shacktown's own Buck

Reinhardt, had all managed to say a few words to the crowd between signing autographs, and Mayor Bondurant had officially declared the Mollie Tucker Owen Community Center open.

A bandstand was hastily improvised inside, and soon the rafters were literally ringing with the music of a loud, fast string band and the sound of some hundred and fifty people having a wonderful time.

Mounds of barbecue and trays of baked beans and slaw were transported from tent to building under umbrellas, and Billy was everywhere, seeing that no harm was done to "Miss Hope's" building. He reported back to her, rather than to Tucker, and Tucker, noticing this, decided to let it pass. The boy had obviously fallen hard. Nothing Tucker could say to him was going to make a difference—the poor kid would just have to work it out the best way he could.

Hope soon dismissed her young assistants so that they could go and enjoy the dancing. Mothers had piled plates high with food and migrated quite naturally toward the child-care area, where they made themselves as comfortable as possible with the child-size furniture. Gossiping, they ate and fed their offspring while Hope moved among them, seeing that everyone had everything they needed. A few extra napkins here, a bib there, and a mop-up whenever and wherever necessary. She was gaining an invaluable insight into how the various children related to their families and to other children, which would in turn give her a handle on how to deal with them once they came under her care.

Hope was elated. This was exactly the way it should be—the women should feel that they had a real stake in the center. For their own sakes, as well as for Tucker's sake, she wanted it to be more than just a place where they dropped off their children while they worked. More than half of them were subsidized by Social Services, and already she had spotted one or two who weren't and probably should have been.

She sighed, understanding all too well how hard it was to ask for help. When pride was all a woman had, she didn't dare risk losing it. For all their difference in background, Hope knew she had far more in common with these women here today than she had with any of her parents' so-called friends at the Brendell's dinner party on Wednesday night.

As she made another trip to the cleaning closet for something to mop up spilled juice, she wondered if Pete and Elsie's guests knew how transparent they had all been. Every single one of them had been dying of curiosity about her in-laws. About what had happened to cause them to move north so suddenly. And what had happened since.

They'd been avid to know how much of the Phillips money she had brought back to Princetown with her. Hope, who considered herself the least sophisticated woman in the world, had been amused at their transparency.

"—Hope, honey, if you're looking for a house, and of course we all know you're anxious to get back here where you belong, why then, Albert Briggs can show you a marvelous place that's just come on the market. Albert, come over her a minute, will you, dear?—"

And John Quincy Marshall III, who happened to be Elsie Brendell's first cousin on her mother's side—and who had collected Hope when her car wouldn't start—also happened to be head of the finest firm of financial advisors in Virginia, and Danville was just a hop, skip and a jump away.

Not a single one of them had made more than a perfunctory inquiry about her parents. She'd been sorely tempted to tell them that between poor Daisy's terminal illness and Hugh's eighteen months of hospitalization and two and a half more years of nursing care—not to mention the money Bob Ed had spent on his second wife six months after Daisy had died—there wasn't enough of the Phillips lumber money left to keep a cat in sardines.

Or if there was, Hope certainly didn't have it.

They'd asked about her wedding, and Hope had been tempted to tell them. But, of course, she never would. When the call had come nearly a year after the Phillipses had moved away that Hugh had been involved in a serious accident, Hope had been as concerned as anyone else. But she'd been shocked rather than concerned when her parents had joined Hugh's in insisting that she go to Boston to be with him.

She had tried to explain that she and Hugh had never been all *that* close, despite the fact that they'd lived next door and dated sporadically. To her knowledge, Hugh had never dated another girl, but that didn't mean he was in love with her.

And she certainly had never pretended to be in love with him. When it came to standing up to authority, however, Hope was a dead loss. She had been almost nineteen years old at the time, still living at home, and like the good little girl she had always strived to be, still subject to her father's complete authority.

"He keeps asking for Hope," Daisy had said over the phone to Hope's mother. "Allie, it's just breaking my heart—you've got to make her come. I—" She had sobbed for a moment, and Allie Outlaw had murmured soothingly, all the while pinning Hope to the spot with one of her *looks*.

"She says poor Hugh keeps begging to see you, honey. They don't even know how long he'll last. The doctors don't hold out a shred of hope, poor boy. Oh, honey, we've got to go. Your daddy and I are going, of course. You know how your daddy feels about ministering to his flock, even when the flock moves on to greener pastures."

In retrospect, Hope wondered if the new wing on the Sunday school building, donated by Phillips Enterprises, had anything to do with her father's devotion to that particular member of his flock.

Guiltily, she pushed the thought out of her mind as unworthy. Her father was a wonderful, caring minister. It wasn't his fault that Hope had eventually let herself be talked into going through a farcical bedside ceremony. At least not entirely.

After practically living at Hugh's bedside for three weeks—her mother's suggestion so that poor Daisy could get some rest, because even though they hadn't known it at the time, Daisy had been ill even then—Hope's sense of proportion, indeed, her sense of reality, had been distorted enough that it had seemed perfectly reasonable.

Her father had performed the service, with both mothers weeping copiously, and half the floor nurses weeping in the hallway. The announcement had come out in the paper the next day, making no mention of the circumstances of the ceremony.

The bride, with a numb and shattered look on her face, had worn a rumpled pink cotton shirtwaist that had been slept in and looked it. The groom had worn a body cast, several miles of gauze and two IV units. Afterward, Hope had listened while four people had tried to convince her that she was making Hugh's few remaining days so much happier.

He hadn't looked happy. She certainly hadn't felt it.

What none of them had realized at the time was that the few days would drag into four heartbreaking years—that Hope's parents would be called to a charge on the other side of the state, and that Hugh's parents would be caught up in the tragedy of his mother's illness and death, leaving Hope to bear the brunt, both financially and emotionally.

"Miss Hope? Miss Hope, it's raining in the window on the fourth floor, and the door's locked, and I can't find nobody that's got a key—"

"Oh—Billy!" It took Hope several seconds to come back to her surroundings. Quickly, she laid aside the uneaten half of her sandwich, signaling Gabby to take over, and hurried out to the stairwell.

"I think the painters must've left it open," Billy offered.

"I expect so. Billy, would you see if you can get hold of Tucker on that radio of yours? I've got a bunch of keys, but I might not have a key to the fourth floor." The small square tower room had once held the water supply for the factory's sprinkler system. It was the only floor that was not scheduled to go into service right away, but it had been renovated along with the rest as it was cheaper and less disruptive to do it then than to bring the contractor back later.

The elevators had not yet been inspected, and Tucker had locked them all and kept the only keys as a safety precaution. By the time Hope had raced up three flights of stairs, her shirt was sticking to her back, and her once-neat hair had come loose and was sticking to her face.

"Oh, botheration," she muttered, clinking through the half dozen keys on the ring she'd been given. All the main areas had locks, and each person had been given a side door key and a key to their particular area. In Hope's case, there were also keys to the gate in the chain-link fence, to the kitchenette, and to Gabby's office, which was locked separately. Only the restrooms, the lobby and the large cleaning closet were left unlocked.

She had tried them all to no avail when she heard the footsteps coming up from the third floor. She knew who it was, of course. That firm, deliberate tread—the soft-soled moccasins he always wore...

"Tucker, I don't have a—"

"God, what happened to *you*?" The minute the words left his tongue, he could have kicked himself.

She bristled. "Nothing happened to me! Now, do you want to let me in there to shut those windows, or do you want to go downstairs and start shoving buckets under leaks?"

It was raining hard, blowing in horizontal sheets against the front of the building. If the windows had been left open, and obviously they had— Dammit, he should have noticed. He should have checked after the painters had gone, but he'd been so intent on avoiding a certain woman, who had been here practically morning, noon and night for the past week—!

He unlocked the door, and they went through the opening at the same time, Tucker taking the front windows,

Hope doing those on the opposite wall. They met on the northeast side, where she was struggling with a particularly stubborn one.

"Darned—stubborn—thing!" she grunted as she threw all her weight on the freshly painted sash.

He lifted her bodily aside and shut the window with comparative ease. And then he turned to see her rubbing her hands together. "Lemme see," he muttered, capturing her hands in his and turning them palm up. "Dammit, I told you you had no business—"

"There's nothing to see!" She tried to snatch them back.

Tucker felt the familiar reaction to the touch of her flesh. Her fragile wrists were no bigger than two of his fingers put together, the underneath surface shadowed with blue veins. "Why the devil didn't you send for me right off instead of trying to do everything yourself?"

"Oh, so now you think closing a few windows is beyond my meager talents?" She tugged at her wrists, but he refused to release her.

"Well, look at you! Your hair's all messed up and you've got a scratch on your cheek—"

"Neither of which is apt to prove fatal," she snapped.

"You could get blood poisoning!"

"Oh, for pity's sake, one of the children grabbed an umbrella before I could get them put away. It's nothing."

"You could have been seriously injured."

"Tucker, I am not a child!"

"And your clothes—have you had a good look at yourself lately?"

She did now. "So? My shirttail's come loose. Big deal! So maybe I have a few smudges here and there—I hardly think—"

"You're a mess! You've got no business trying to keep up with that crew of hellions, and you know it! I told you right off this wasn't going to work, Hope. You don't belong over here—it's not your kind of place."

She stared at him in amazement. "Do you know you sound just like my mother? My *mother*, for goodness' sake!"

"Okay, so we're both trying to protect you. It's not exactly a crime, you know," he said defensively. He was still holding her, but somehow, it felt different. His fingers were no longer manacles—his thumbs caressed the thin skin of her inner wrists, and then strayed further up her arm, while his eyes never left hers.

Dark eyes today. She had seen them as clear as a summer sky, but when he was agitated, or angry, or—excited over something—they turned the color of sunwarmed slate.

He was angry. "Tucker, you don't seem to understand that I have to earn a living. I'm not a dependent child any longer, you know. Maybe working in a project like this isn't going to make me rich, but it's something I've always wanted to do. It's what I know *how* to do, and what's more, I don't need—"

"You don't know what you need," he growled. "That much is obvious. If you did, you wouldn't be here."

"Oh, no? And where would I be? Sitting on a silk cushion up in some turret in a River Ridge castle? Living on butterfly milk and nectar? Fat chance!" She wrenched her wrists from his grip, and glared at him, and Tucker glared right back.

"I told you I was going to take care of you one day! Didn't I tell you that? Why the hell couldn't you have waited for me? I was doing just fine—I would've been able to buy you a good enough house—maybe not on River Ridge, but there are other places just as good. Better!"

Her face seemed to crumple right before his eyes, and Tucker felt as if someone had sucker-punched him. "Aaahh, sweetheart, don't—please don't."

She was in his arms so fast her first tears soaked into his shirt before they could fall. He could feel her sobs, feel how hard she was trying to control them. Hope had never let him see her cry—not since she was a child, and then only rarely. For all he knew, she'd never let *anyone* see her cry.

"Look, sweetheart, whatever it is, I can fix it. I promise you, I'll do everything in my power, but—aaahh, baby." He rocked her against him as she cried harder. Her arms were around his neck, her slight body plastered hard against his, until he was barely hanging onto his sanity.

Oh, no! Don't let it happen to me now—please! For the first time in seven years, she needs me. If I go and get horny now, it's gonna ruin everything!

Gradually, the sobbing diminished until it was only the occasional sniffle and hiccup. Tucker held her tightly, but not too tightly. He didn't want to alarm her. He had turned himself so that she was more or less braced against his hipbone, which should keep her from becoming aware of any undue activity in the immediate area.

After awhile, her hands slipped down to his shoulders and she shoved herself away. He didn't release her—not entirely. "Better now?" he asked in his most comforting tone of voice.

"I can't imagine what made me do that." She smiled, her eyes red-rimmed and swollen, her nose red, and her pale lipstick smudged—probably onto his shirt. She was as beautiful as an October sunrise on the river. Damp, foggy, colorful, and utterly irresistible. His own little princess.

"I can. You've been going at it day and night this past week. Honey, you shouldn't be working so hard. You're not cut out for that."

Her red, pink and brown eyes widened, and she said, "Tucker Owen, wash your mouth out with soap! For as long as I can remember you've talked about wanting a place on this side of the river where children could play, and adults could take classes, and—and people could feel like they really belonged to something besides drudgery and poverty and—and I am *so* cut out for it. If you can do it, I can do it!"

"Well, yeah, but—"

"But you think I'm made out of crystal, right? One sharp rap and I've had it? Tucker, you know what your trouble is? You're a snob! A male chauvinist *snob*! You've managed to pull this thing together for the people over here, and you want to think you've done it all by your macho self—you think you and a few of your macho racy friends did the whole blessed thing! Well, it's just not true, and what's more, it's not fair!"

"That's rac*ing*. Not racy. And you're talking crazy, lady, because without a few Ridgebacks, such as your friend Brendell and old Harrington, we'd be standing here in a moldering old rat heap with rain coming through the roof like it was made out of paper. Another few years and the whole place would have been bulldozed to make way for a sewage treatment plant or something. So where do you get off saying—" He broke off, peering closely at her face as she covered her left eye with her hand. "Hope? What is it?"

"Nothing—something's in my eye, that's all."

"Let me see." He tried to move her hand, but she refused to be helped. Typical. How the hell had she gotten so damned independent all of a sudden? The old Hope would have come to him right off and asked him to fix it for her.

"Oh, shoot—Tucker, see if you can see anything."

Her face was between his hands, and her breath was warm on his cheeks, and when she suddenly blinked and said, "There—I think it floated out," he didn't release her.

There was no way on God's green earth he could keep from kissing her then, and once he kissed her, there would be no way he could keep from wanting her so bad it ate into him like battery acid.

She was in his system—always had been. Probably always would be. But he could handle it. He *had* to. Tucker told himself he was no longer a green kid with too many dreams and not enough brains. He knew precisely how far he could go without risking everything. He knew how to hold back, he assured himself. Half throttle and no more.

He would go a little way—just far enough to keep him sane—and then he'd ease back.

"Hope, close your eyes," he whispered.

As if she had no will of her own, she did.

Tucker smiled. It was a knowing smile, not one that Hope or anyone else who knew him would have found reassuring.

The moment his lips touched her trembling mouth, he told himself he just might have overestimated his powers of resistance.

But it was too late now.

Seven

Outside, the rain beat against the tower room like a barrage of heavy artillery. Occasional flashes of lightning illuminated the grayness. Inside, the smell of paint competed with the clean scent of Hope's hair. The scent of her skin reminded Tucker, as it always had, of nectarines.

"Oh, sweetheart, I've been...wanting this for so...long," he whispered, the words interspersed with small hungry nibbles at her lips, her chin. From three floors below came the throbbing beat of square dance music. The cadence of his heart was faster, heavier.

She was clinging to him, her body pressed as tightly as possible against his. There was no way he could hide the effect she had on him—he no longer bothered to try.

"I think—hadn't we better—go down?" Hope managed between kisses and gasps of air.

"Probably..." She still hadn't tucked in her shirttail, and now his hands were stroking the smooth, slightly damp skin of her back. The narrow cotton band of her bra contrasted with the satiny texture of her skin.

Not satin—more like velvet, he decided, kissing the vulnerable underside of her jaw.

Beneath her shirt, his hands found their way to her shoulders and cupped the delicate roundness. Then, as slowly as humanly possible under the circumstances, he brought them down to her sides, beneath her arms...and around to the soft swell of her breasts.

He was shaking like a leaf! With a desperate glance around, he led her over to the only piece of furniture in the room—a scaffold left behind by the crew of painters. Swinging her up in his arms, he lowered her until she was sitting on the rough boards. With a hand on each of her knees, he eased them apart and moved closer.

"I wish to God we had someplace better," he said fleetingly. "At least it's a tower, not a dungeon."

"You've always had the wrong idea about me, Tucker."

But he was too busy exploring her throat with his lips to argue. She tasted faintly of soap. She had tasted the same way the first time he had ever kissed her—the clean, wholesome scent of a clean, wholesome...princess.

"I wish we were back at our place," he murmured, his voice thick with emotion as he kissed the gentle slope of her breast and raked the lace-covered tips with his teeth.

"We—we'd probably drown," she managed, laughter bubbling just under the surface. "It's pouring down out there."

"Stop squirming." His voice was muffled against her flesh.

"But I can't reach your zipper without moving."

"Good. My fuse has been burning too long as it is—you go fooling around with zippers, there's no telling what might happen."

"You mean you get to fool around, but I don't? That's not fair."

"Nope. Neither one of us gets to fool around," he said, reluctantly putting her away from him.

"What do you call what we've just been doing?" she asked indignantly.

He had the grace to look embarrassed. "Uh... conditioned reflex?"

"Is that why you followed me up here?"

"I followed you up here, as you put it, because you sent for me to unlock the door. Remember?"

This time, it was Hope who looked embarrassed. So flustered, in fact, that before he had time to think, Tucker caught her to him and buried his grin in her hair. "Yeah, I thought that might get you down off your high horse in a hurry."

"Tucker, why do I always end up making a fool of myself around you?"

He kissed one eyebrow. And because he couldn't help himself, the other one, as well. "Do you, sweet? I'd never noticed."

"All the things I used to tell you—I can't believe I was ever such a..."

"Princess," he whispered, swept back onto the dream he had carried for so long—the dream of one day riding up the manicured slopes of the hill called River Ridge and carrying her off to a place he had made for her—a place that was even finer, even higher. He would have given her a home more beautiful than anything she had ever imagined in her wildest dreams, if he'd had to work three lifetimes to do it.

"I'm not a princess, Tuck... Ahhhh, you know I could never stand it when you did that," she groaned.

He was suckling one of her earlobes. She seldom wore earrings—her mother had never allowed her to have her ears pierced, claiming ladies never did. She shuddered and tried to ease herself from his arms, and he let her go, but only so far.

"Trust me—I have ways of recognizing a real live princess when I happen to run across one." He didn't know if she was aware of it or not, but her fingers were kneading his sides just under his arms, driving him slightly out of his gourd. He couldn't bring himself to stop her.

"You mean like the Princess and the Pea?"

He blinked at that. "The princess and the *what*?"

"You know—the story about the way they discovered who was the real princess by placing a tiny pea under a big stack of mattresses on her bed. The one who complained was the real princess, because a commoner would never have been sensitive enough to feel the lump."

"Oh. Yeah. Well, I don't happen to have a bed handy, and I'm sorrier than I can tell you about that, but trust me— I can tell the real thing anytime." His heart turned over at the sight of her smile that, from the looks of her, could as easily have veered over into tears as into laughter. "It's a God-given talent we commoners have," he said modestly.

She was laughing now, and the sound made *him* feel almost like crying. It was hopeless. *He* was hopeless. "Welcome home, sweetheart," he said softly, and she leaned forward and rested her forehead in the curve of his shoulder.

"Oh, Tucker—thank you."

It was all she could think of to say. The words "welcome home" had never sounded so sweet, and if he meant welcome to my arms—welcome back to my heart—why then, she wasn't about to say anything that would jeopardize that feeling.

God, he smelled so good! Like clean laundry and shaving lotion and toothpaste—and beer and barbecue. He was so supremely good to look at, his eyes so dark in the dim light that they might as well have been black.

"Tucker, I've missed you so much," she whispered, turning her head so that her lips just brushed the side of his throat. She hadn't meant to start anything more, she just needed to be closer to him. "Sometimes I felt so lost...so..." She sighed, and he gathered her to him with a groan, sliding her hips forward until he was pressed against the juncture of her thighs.

It was like an explosion. Torch to tinder. She felt him swell and harden against her, and for a moment, she was back on the riverbank, on that summer afternoon so long ago when they had almost . . .

She drew in a deep, shuddering breath through her open mouth. Her hands slipped from his shoulders and moved down his chest, parting his shirt.

Tucker gasped as her fingertips raked over his nipples, and encouraged, she returned and caressed them until he was trembling all over.

His arms slipped from around her, grasping her wrists, and he held her hands away from his body. "Sweetheart—please, you don't know what you're doing," he said hoarsely.

"Then show me," she pleaded. "Tucker, please—I need you."

In his shock, he released her wrists, and she lifted her hands to the buttons on her shirt. Before he realized what she was doing, she had unfastened them all and released the last two buttons on his.

"Hope, stop this! You don't know what you're doing. Honey, we can't—you can't—"

"Why not?"

Groaning, he held her against him and stared over her head at the driving rain. This was crazy! This wasn't supposed to be happening. Not this way—not at all! "Honey—Hope, listen to me. You can't just barge back into my life and—and—" *Have your way with me.* The words sounded in his mind, the thought so ludicrous that he began to chuckle.

And then, still holding her, his chin resting on top of her head, he began to laugh. What the hell—it was better than crying.

"I hate you," she said, her voice muffled against his bare chest.

"No, you don't. I wish to hell you did."

She began to struggle, and he released her. She was furious, embarrassed. She turned away and began buttoning her shirt. Maybe he should have taken what she offered after all, he thought, watching her quick, angry actions. At least he might have gotten her out of his system that way.

"Stop looking at me, damn you!"

"I like looking at you. I always have."

"But from a safe distance, right? Not so close you might accidentally be forced into some sort of a commitment, right?"

She was coming apart, and watching her, Tucker wanted to—

But he couldn't, dammit! It wouldn't solve anything.

Stepping back, he studied her once-smooth hair that the midday stubble on his jaw had brushed into unruliness. He took in the two bright patches of uneven color on her cheeks, the suspicious brilliance of her dark eyes, and felt his own anger and frustration drain away. "Sweetheart, the floor's dusty. There's not a stick of furniture up here, not even a sprig of honeysuckle."

He tried for a whimsical smile, but whimsy had never been his long suit. When he saw her trying to wriggle down off the platform, he reached for her again.

She flinched from his hands. "I can manage, thank you."

"You'll get a splinter in your—ah, skirt."

"Don't worry about it, I'll have one of the peasants remove it for me."

"Don't be bitter, honey—it doesn't become you."

Her jaw fell, and she stared at him. "Would you mind going straight to hell?"

Tucker had seen her in a temper before, but never quite this way. The red patches were gone, leaving her face pale, but her eyes still glittered feverishly. They were moist, and he knew that if she cried, she would never forgive herself. Or him.

"It's just not the right place, Hope. Or the right time."

"Oh, sorry—remind me to make a proper appointment with you next time."

His jaw tightened. He could feel a nerve twitching at his temple. Making a deliberate effort to speak calmly, he said, "I reckon we'd better go downstairs and see how the floor's holding up." The steady thump-thump of a noisy group of square dancers and an enthusiastic band could be heard all the way to the tower room. "Wonder how much longer this thing's going to last. We didn't think to set a closing time."

Hope used the small space to tidy her clothes, although Tucker had to forcefully stop himself from tucking the back of her shirttail in and smoothing her hair away from her face.

God, would it never end—the hold she had on him?

"Speaking of closing time," she said, in a voice that was commendably close to normal, "I'm going to have to leave early. I've made arrangements with Gabby and the girls to cover for me."

He frowned. "What's the trouble? Do you need any help?"

The look she sent him was as regal as any royal princess. "I believe I can manage quite well, thank you."

"Manage what?"

"The rain's stopped. Do you think we should open the windows again so that it can dry out in—"

"Manage what, Hope? If you've got a problem—"

"My only problem is that I can't seem to convince you that I no longer need you meddling in my affairs—if I ever did."

Hope knew the moment she uttered the words that she'd gone too far. She edged toward the door, fumbling for the heavy brass handle.

"If—you—ever—did?" he repeated, stalking her.

She made an unsuccessful attempt at a laugh. "Sorry if I stepped on your ego, but—"

"Don't worry, lady, my ego's been kicked around by bigger boots than yours. You didn't even leave a footprint on it."

"Fine. Then if that's all settled, I'll be going."

"You wanna go? Go. I never expected you to stick it out, but I thought at least you might last through the opening ceremony."

Hope's five-feet-six had never looked so tall. Head high, she said, "I've always considered sarcasm a despicable weapon."

"Your shirttail's out in back."

With a stifled exclamation, she spun around, jamming her shirt in with both hands. Seeing the color flare in her face again, it was all he could do not to catch her in his arms. God, what was it about this one woman that she could knock the pins right out from under him with a single look?

"Go on downstairs, honey—I'll lock up here," he said, sorry he'd ragged her. Sorry he'd touched her. Sorry he hadn't made love to her seven years ago, when he'd been crazy enough to believe there was a chance for them.

"Thanks, I—thanks," she said, and slipped out through the heavy door, leaving him feeling angry, frustrated and lost.

Leaving him *feeling*. There was the trouble. Tucker didn't want to feel—not where Hope was concerned. Because in spite of everything, he still loved her so much it was killing him. Once, a long time ago, he'd been too young and too stubborn to realize that there wasn't a snowflake's chance for a guy like him and a girl like her.

Nothing had changed. It wasn't in him to deny his background. He'd stopped trying to outrun his roots a long time ago—about seven years ago, to be exact. And Hope Phillips, wealthy young widow, didn't fit into that background any better now than she had when she'd been Hope Outlaw, the princess of River Ridge.

Tucker waited a few minutes, and then he went back down to join in the festivities. He'd never felt less festive in his life. He was just in time to see Hope emerge from Gabby's office, her hair smoothly rebraided and her lips bright with the shade of lipstick Gabby habitually wore.

He continued to watch as she hurried out through the side door, dodging puddles, and climbed into the Jaguar. Then, his eyes as bleak as January rain, he crossed the room and asked Miss Polly to dance.

Hope waved to Billy, who stood forlornly outside the gate. He'd offered to jump-start her Honda for her, but she hadn't wanted to wait in case Tucker saw her. John Quincy had driven up with Elsie Brendell just as she was grinding her starter for the tenth time, and he'd offered her a lift.

"Thanks—I could use one. Just let me say goodbye to someone," and she'd hurried over to Billy and asked him to keep in touch with Gabby in case she needed anything.

"Sure. See you tomorrow, Miss Hope. Don't worry none about that mess them kids made on the floor. I'll clean it up for you."

"Billy, we have someone to mop the floors, but thanks anyway. I don't know what we would've done without you today."

The boy beamed. And blushed. Hope wondered for the first time if there could possibly be anything in what Gabby had said—that Billy had a crush on her.

"Thanks again." She went to rejoin John Quincy. Once settled in the car, she glanced over her shoulder to see him still standing there staring after her. Oh, Lordy, couldn't anything in life be simple?

"Sounds like they're having quite a time in there," John Quincy observed, and Hope turned her attention to him, grateful for the distraction. He was a nice man. Almost too nice. He had been rather insistent about seeing her again the night he'd brought her home from Elsie's dinner party, but once she'd made him understand, ever so tactfully, that she wasn't looking for a man and she had no money to invest in anything larger than a new battery for her car—no matter what he'd been led to believe—he had backed off graciously enough.

"Would you like to go somewhere for a drink?"

"Thanks, John Quincy, but I'd better get home. Today's my mother's birthday, and I wanted to call her. Sometimes it takes a while to get through."

"Wanda, you got a minute? Something I'd like to talk over with you." Tucker waited outside the screen door while a radio was turned off and a cat was ordered off the couch.

"It's about Billy, isn't it? Lawsy, I knew it! He hasn't been home a single day in over a week."

"Yeah—well, it's not exactly about Billy. I mean, he's okay if that's what you're worried about."

She laughed bitterly, looking both too young and too old to be the same age as Tucker. They'd been in school together before Wanda had dropped out. "Thing number one," she said in a soft, raspy drawl. "You know what they say—take a number and wait? That's what I tell my worries when they gang up on me. C'mon inside, I'll fix you a glass of ice tea. Shoo, Thomas, you get out of that flowerpot 'fore I whomp you good!"

They sat and sipped for a few minutes, and Tucker glanced around. Wanda's house was about the same age as his, and in about the same shape his had been before he'd overhauled it. The first thing it needed was a new roof. After that, some new flooring where damp rot had set in, and—

He broke off. Dammit, he couldn't rebuild the whole neighborhood single-handedly. Sooner or later people were going to have to start taking some responsibility for themselves.

At least he could offer her some hope—a place to start. "Look, I don't know if you've been down to look over that old place on the corner of Plum and Haggarty. We've turned it into sort of a community center."

Wanda rocked steadily in a bentwood chair that looked out of place among the battered chrome and vinyl furniture. She placed the cold wet glass against the side of her neck and waited for him to continue.

Now that he was here, Tucker didn't quite know what to say. He pretended a great interest in his surroundings while he tried to pull his thoughts together. There were plants everywhere—red flowers, white flowers, yellow ones and some green feathery looking thing with no blooms at all. "They're, uh—real pretty, aren't they?" He nodded to the indoor garden, which took up every available surface and overflowed onto the floor.

"This community place of yours—Billy said it was real nice. He's been hanging around there a lot lately, and I want you to know, if he gets into a lick o' trouble, you just send him on home, you hear? He's not got too big for me to take a belt to him if he needs it."

On second thought, maybe helping out at the day-care center wasn't such a hot idea, Tucker mused. Still, there had to be something for her there—some kind of a job that would get her back on track before she derailed Billy's life, too.

In desperation, he fell back on the plants. "Umm...what do you call that thing with the bunches of red flowers?"

"Geranium. I got pink, too. Miss Polly gave me that cutting."

"It's real pretty," said Tucker, wondering why he hadn't thought this thing through before he'd come barging in here. Hell, he wasn't even in a position to hire anyone, not personally. It was just that he felt so responsible....

"Well now, I can root most anything that grows, and that's the Lord's truth. Always could. Learned it from my Aunt Etta. See, the trick is, you gotta let it dry out a little bit first instead of just ramming it in the dirt the minute you break it off. I always sprinkle a little baby powder on the cut end, too—makes it set out roots quicker."

"Yeah...I can see how that might work," Tucker said gravely, all the while wondering how he was going to get out of there without sounding like too big a fool. Next time, he'd think first and act later.

"C'mon outside, I'll show you my hydrangeas. I got blue and pink. It's all in the soil, you know. This dirt around here's sour, but you take a handful of lime... Oh, and wait'll you see my zinnias. I got zinnias bigger'n a dishpan. C'mon, bring your ice tea around back, Tucker. I got a bench I made out of a plank and some concrete blocks that's real nice to sit on once the sun gets low enough."

Tucker had said about all he could think of to say about her flowers, but he didn't have the heart to go off and leave her when she looked so perked up. Maybe she didn't get all that much company—not in the daytime, anyway.

"Yeah, sure, that'd be real nice," he mumbled, following her out through the sagging door, across the sagging front porch and out into a hard-packed, grassless scrap of a yard.

He voiced his admiration for the jungle she had created in her miniscule backyard, sampled one of the early figs from her bush, and made some excuse about needing to go by his office. By the time he found himself at her front gate, which was also sagging, since the supports had long since rotted off, Tucker was beginning to have a germ of an idea. It was a long shot, but it just might work.

"Look, Wanda, don't worry about Billy, hear? He's been helping out down at the center—odd jobs and all. He's real handy. Basically, he's a good kid."

She sighed, her thin shoulders lifting and falling under the bright colored silky print of her dress. Dangling pink rhinestone earrings sparkled against her mouse-colored hair, and for a moment she looked so discouraged that Tucker wanted to promise her that everything would be all right.

But how the hell could he do that? He was no magician. He wasn't even a social worker. And while Billy was a good kid at heart, even good kids could get in trouble, and Billy had some man-size problems to work through.

"Look, I'll be in touch in a few days. I—ah, I've been needing some plants for my place, and we might need some down at the center."

"Roses is having a sale right now. I saw it in the Sunday paper. They got two-gallon size—"

"Yeah, well—I mean something more like what you've got. Germanius and those ferny looking things—what'd you call 'em?"

"Ferns. And it's ge*ran*iums, not ger*man*ius, but anyway, you're welcome to cuttings off anything I've got, Tucker. I'll even root 'em for you."

"Yeah, sure—that'd be real nice." He backed a few steps down the broken sidewalk.

"Tucker, about Billy," Wanda said, and for the first time Tucker could see the strong resemblance to her son under all the makeup, "I sure do thank you for all the—well, for all the time you spent on him. A boy needs a man—Billy's not got any man to look up to, and—well, I just thank you, that's all."

"Yeah, well...you were real good to Mama when she was sick, Wanda. Reckon that's what friends and neighbors are for."

He escaped just as a light blue Ford pulled up in front of her house. Climbing into his own car, Tucker caught a glimpse of the look on Wanda's face as she waited for her company. She looked tired, he thought—tired and discouraged. As if someone had turned off the light that had burned inside her a few minutes before.

"'Lo, Harold," she said, and he thought she sounded tired, too. "You're early."

Tucker was restless. For the past week, he'd been edgy as hell, for no good reason. He'd baked two pound cakes and a bunch of peanut butter cookies, but not even that had done the trick. He'd passed them out around the neighborhood and got a sack of summer squash and another one of cucumbers and tomatoes in return.

Okay, let's line 'em up, tackle 'em one at a time, he told himself. The center? It'd been open for a week and a half now, and from all reports, was going great.

The new fuel bowl? It had proved itself at Daytona. He had two firms interested, and another possible. No problem there.

There was Wanda, of course. Not really his problem, but he'd thought if he could get her started in something that would bring in some money and engage her interests, Billy would quit going off like a firecracker every few weeks.

And there was Billy himself. In spite of all his careful planning—or maybe because of it—the kid was headed for another batch of trouble unless he missed his guess. He needed to get him away from the center—away from Hope—before the poor kid got hurt too bad.

He swore softly. Instead of turning off on Pokeberry, he turned onto Haggarty and headed for the center. He hadn't been back since the grand opening—since the day he'd made such a jackass of himself up there in the tower.

He couldn't stay away forever. He'd figured she'd have gotten tired and quit by now, but from what he heard from the neighborhood kids, Miss Hope was a cross between the good fairy and the angel on top of the Christmas tree.

Hell, he could've told them that.

Eight

Hope was standing beside her car, a forgotten pencil jammed in her braid, arms crossed over her chest, when Tucker pulled into the center's parking lot. It was nearly six, and he happened to know that the last child was usually collected by five, or shortly after.

There wasn't another car in the lot, and he pulled up beside her. "Waiting for someone?" he asked, trying his damnedest to sound casual when casual was the last thing he was feeling.

"No."

When she didn't elaborate, he tented his eyebrows and said, "So? You planning on camping out here tonight?"

"I'm cooling off," she said, and snapped her mouth shut again.

Crossed arms, jutting chin, flashing eyes. "Something's bugging you, right?"

"You could say that. In fact you could say that any car that fails to start three days out of four deserves whatever happens to it, and right now, ax-murder doesn't sound at all excessive!''

"Gabby mentioned you'd been having some trouble." In fact, she had pinned it down to the battery, if Tucker remembered correctly. And he usually did—at least where automobiles were concerned.

He'd tried to arrange for one of his men to go over the thing, but Hope had refused point-blank, and he'd known better than to push.

Hope dragged in a deep breath and blew it up over her face, sending her hair dancing around her forehead. It was hot, humid, and utterly still. She looked as bedraggled as it's possible for a beautiful woman to look when she's had charge of twenty-three young hellions all day.

"I'm finished for the day, so I may as well give you a lift. Looks like we might be in for another thunderstorm tonight." He had opened the door of his car and turned so that one long leg stretched out onto the graveled surface and one arm hung casually over the steering wheel. He could as easily have offered to jump-start her car, since he carried a set of cables in every vehicle he owned.

Hope sighed and looked at the sky, which had turned a brassy shade of nothing, with dark gray moving up rapidly from the southwest. And then she looked at him. "If you're sure you don't mind," she said grudgingly. "Could we stop by a garage so that I can send someone out here?"

"I'll handle it," he said, fully expecting to be shot down for his offer. She didn't disappoint him.

"I'm perfectly capable of—"

"Look, do you want a lift, or don't you? It's going to storm like hell in a minute."

With a look that would have curdled milk, she came around and let herself in. As much as it went against the grain, he didn't get out and offer to help her in. Instead, he sat there like a clod and tried to hide his feeling of triumph over sidestepping her arguments. There were times when a guy had to fight dirty.

"How'd it go today?" he asked with seeming casualness.

"Pretty good. The usual scraps and scratches. Nothing a little hug and a bandage won't cure, so far."

"How're your part-timers working out?"

"The girls? Jenny's already gone. The other two are talking about getting a job waiting tables. I don't think we'll have them much longer." Her sigh seemed dredged up from the soles of her feet, and it was all Tucker could do not to reach over and pull her against him. "I guess I could start tipping them after juice and cookies. I think they're a little disappointed that they're not getting rich."

"I'll look into it," Tucker murmured.

"There's nothing to look into. Besides, we've got everything under control, honestly. I'm just feeling—oh, I don't know...I think it's the weather."

"You can't handle that bunch alone."

"I don't. Gabby comes in an hour after I do and takes over while I have a break. She watches the nappers while the others are out on the playground, and Billy Coe is usually around if we get in a bind."

"I'll check it out," he promised, and Hope shot him a disgruntled look.

"You missed the turn-off," she said several minutes later.

"I wanted to show you something first—You've got a minute, haven't you?"

It was a crazy idea and he knew it. The minute she discovered where he was taking her, she would either demand that he drive her home or conk him over the head, steal his keys and drive herself. With this new, independent Hope, he wasn't sure what to expect.

By the time he pulled up in front of the neat yellow house with the green shutters and the green front door, Tucker had pretty well figured out the approach he was going to take. He'd practically kidnapped the woman; it wasn't going to help matters if he came on to her like a half-starved wolf. One thing he'd discovered over the past two years—under all that expensive polish, most Ridgebacks had a pretty active social conscience. It galled him to admit it, after resenting them all these years, but what the hell—he wasn't above using it. And right now, it might be exactly the right tack to take.

"So, what do you think—this neighborhood has possibilities, right? You take this place here—hard to believe that a few years back it was nothing more than a tar-paper shack. The roof was so swaybacked you could've thrown a saddle on it and ridden the damned thing, and as for the windows, half of 'em were covered with scraps of plywood or sheet metal—whatever my old man could scrounge."

"This was yours?"

"Is mine," he corrected, making no move to get out of the car.

"Tucker, you don't have to—"

"No, that's okay—I just thought as long as you were working over here, you might as well get to know the neighborhood." He waited, ready to counter her next move, and when it didn't come, he spent a few seconds appreciating the quiet purr of the powerhouse under his hood, and then he switched off the engine. "I just wanted you to know what we're up against over here, Hope. There've been some improvements, but on the whole, it's a pretty rough area. The center was a good start, but if you're going to be working in this part of town, you may as well start understanding it."

At this point, Tucker didn't know whether he was trying to sell her on the place or scare her away. Maybe he was trying to tell her something about himself. Shacktown was a part of him. He couldn't change that, and he'd long since stopped trying to deny his heritage—such as it was. He might clean it up, but he damned well wasn't going to deny it.

"So—what about it? You game for the grand tour? Takes about thirty-five seconds flat from start to finish, and the admission's free on rainy Tuesday evenings." The angle of his head was arrogant. The look in his eyes was not. "Unless you're hungry, that is. Then it might take longer, because I've got a slow-cooker going in the kitchen with boiled ham, string beans and potatoes, and in the refrigerator there's about seven-sixteenths of my famous chocolate-coconut-cherry cheesecake with a peanut butter crust."

Evidently he'd sent her into deep shock. Taking advantage of the situation, Tucker was out and around to her side of the car in no time at all. He handed her out onto the carefully swept dirt sidewalk—he paid a neighborhood kid five bucks a week to keep it spotless.

Not giving her a chance to come to her senses, he took her arm and propelled her toward his front porch. "Now on your right and left you'll see as nice a patch of grass as you'll find on any golf course. There's this sod company about three hours' drive from here, and they laid it down for me in one morning. Next I thought I'd go for some flowers. You know—germanius and stuff like that."

He checked for a reaction. She wasn't dragging her feet, but she wasn't exactly turning cartwheels of joy, either. He was going to have to keep it strictly impersonal. If it killed him.

"You see before you a set of genuine wood porch furniture, including a swing that's got just the right amount of squeak to keep you from dozing off and falling out—and a yellow light by the door. That's supposed to keep mosquitoes from going inside your house, but mine use the back door. They're not proud."

"It's uh—lovely," Hope said weakly. It was the first time she'd spoken since they'd arrived. On the other hand, he'd been hitting on all eight cylinders ever since he'd got her in the car. Maybe if he shut up long enough, she could squeeze in a few words. Such as why the hell had he brought her there and when was he taking her home.

Tucker tensed, ready to start talking her out of leaving. "Hold on, you haven't seen anything yet." Without releasing her arm, he unlocked the door and held it wide. "In your neck of the woods, it's called a foyer. Over here we call it a front hall. On the right is the master bedroom...." He opened the door just wide enough to give her a glimpse of a king-size bed and a dark pine dresser, and then shut it again. Thank God he'd made the bed before he'd left for work this morning. And for once, there were no shirts hanging from the bedpost.

Hope made some noncommittal sound, and Tucker tried to contain the sheer joy of seeing her in his home—no matter if he had had to kidnap her and bring her here against her will.

"Guest room on the left, and then we come to the sitting room, otherwise known as the back parlor—actually, it's the front one, too—it's the only parlor I have. Which leads directly into the bathroom and kitchen without the messy business of having to plow through a bunch of dining room furniture. Efficiency—that's what it's all about. My architect tells me this is the house of the future."

He had noticed the beginning of a smile earlier, and looked away quickly, afraid it would be a smile of derision. Now she was openly laughing. Cautiously, he leaned his shoulders up against the kitchen door frame and watched to see which way she was going to jump once she sobered up. God, how long had it been since he'd heard her laugh? It had always surprised him, because she was such a delicate, ladylike creature, and her laughter was deep and gurgling and full-bodied. He used to love her laughter. He used to love everything about her.

To his everlasting chagrin, he still did.

"Do you mind my asking who your architect was?" she asked, daintily blotting the corners of her eyes.

He shrugged. "Me. Architect, general contractor and carpenter. I'd have done the plumbing and electrical stuff, too, but they have these crazy rules that say you've got to know what you're doing before they'll allow you to wire up a house or install a john."

"Absurd," Hope declared, the echo of laughter lingering in her voice. She fell silent, her gaze focused absently on
a blue bowl containing an orange, a banana and a pocket
calculator.

"What are you thinking?" he dared.

It was her turn to sigh now, and she did. "I was remembering the way you used to tease me about my table manners. You taught me so much, Tucker."

Embarrassed, he turned and straightened a picture on the
wall. It was of Richard Petty leaning against his famous
number forty-three. Hope noticed that it was autographed
with a personal and rather irreverent message to Tuck Owen.

"I didn't teach you anything," he said gruffly. "Hell, I
didn't know a salad fork from a ball-joint fork."

She shook her head, a smile still lingering in her eyes.
"You taught me things my mother should have taught me,
and you did it without once embarrassing me. When I think
about it now, I can't imagine how I ever went to you with
such things as . . . well . . . anyway, you were wonderful. I'll
always appreciate it."

"That sounds suspiciously like a farewell speech."

"It isn't," she assured him. "I know you don't believe
me, Tucker, but I'm here to stay." It was spoken almost as
a dare. Hope was wondering why he had brought her
there—whether he had finally made up his mind what, if
anything, he wanted from her.

She knew what she wanted from him. It was the same
thing she'd always wanted—his love. Looking at him now,
his hair still as thick and dark as ever, but his face leaner, his
eyes more veiled, it was not hard to picture the man he had
been seven years ago—or even seventeen years ago, for he'd
been a man when most males were boys.

It had been Tucker who had taught her to laugh at life's
little absurdities. It had been Tucker who had scolded her
for swearing once when she'd been mad as the devil and too
stubborn to cry. He'd given her a word to use instead, and
it had been so ludicrous that from then on, whenever she got

angry, she thought of the word and wanted to laugh, instead.

It had been Tucker who, with his great strength and his tough gentleness, had always made her feel so cherished, so protected . . . so loved.

"Tucker, what happened to us?" she whispered, and then she went cold. The words had slipped out before she could recall them.

Tucker stiffened as if he'd taken a blow to the belly. His eyes narrowed, and he saw her take a step back. "I think it's pretty obvious, isn't it? Sorry things turned out the way they did—for both of us."

They were standing in the center of his spotless kitchen, which had been painted white—even the floor was white. There was a yellow Crockpot simmering on one of the wooden cabinets, and a bird feeder outside the window over the sink was doing a land-office business.

"Would you like to go into the parlor?" Without waiting he led the way, and she followed the few steps to the comfortable living area.

It, too, had been painted white, the floors sanded and refinished. There were no pictures on the walls here—no curtains at the windows anywhere, but the furniture was good. Plain, mostly browns and beige in leather and tweed.

"What happened?" he repeated. "I think it's pretty clear, isn't it? No point in plowing through old history."

"I wrote. You never answered," she said, standing awkwardly just inside the door. They needed to talk, if only to clear the air between them, but now that the time had arrived, she didn't know what to say—how much to tell him.

"That would be about the time I left on the Alaska job. Some of the mail was forwarded, some of it's probably still floating around, trying to catch up with me."

"After seven years?" she asked faintly.

His expression said he neither knew nor cared. "Like I told you, your folks filled me in on all I needed to know."

"Tucker, please—I'd like to tell you about it."

"Honey, the last thing I need or want is a rehash of one of your old romances. I've got enough of my own to keep straight."

Seeing her chin lift that telling fraction of an inch, Tucker could have kicked himself. He had the pride of a Ridgeback and the brains of a jackass. It was a bad combination.

"Sit down before you drop," he said gruffly.

"If you don't mind, I'd rather go—"

"Sit!"

She moved toward a chair that had been scaled to Tucker's size and lowered herself carefully. Hands clasped in her lap, she stared at him. Her eyes, all shadows and yearnings, tore him apart.

"So?" he prompted. "You wanted to talk—talk."

For a full minute, she said nothing. And then, drawing a deep breath, she spoke. "Hugh was involved in an accident."

Tucker nodded thoughtfully. "I heard something about it—not much. Was it before or after you went to Boston?"

"Before. Actually, that's why I went."

He waited for her to continue, torn between wanting to know and not wanting to know.

"Tucker, I was eighteen years old—nearly nineteen, but I had never lived on my own, never been allowed to make my own decisions, and—and I didn't even have sense enough to realize how immature I was. You've always been so independent, you can have no idea what it's like, trying to live your life according to someone else's directions."

"You're telling me it was your folks' idea, marrying Phillips?" When she nodded, he shook his head slowly. "And you just *went along with them*? Honey, I know you had problems being assertive, but—"

"Are you going to let me tell this, or are you going to keep butting in?"

Tucker held up his hands as if to say, the floor's all yours.

"All right, then. When you put it that way, it sounds awful, but you have to understand that Hugh had lived next door ever since we moved to Princetown. We were friends. He used to tell me things he never told anyone else, and that—well, it makes for a certain closeness. They moved away because he'd been involved in some sort of scandal at school—cheating, they said, but I never believed it because Hugh was brilliant. Anyhow, his parents didn't like Craig, his roommate, and I think probably Craig got caught cheating and Hugh tried to protect him, but we'll never know. Craig came to visit Hugh once after that, and Daisy was all upset, and Bob Ed got rid of him. Hugh was furious.''

Tucker listened without comment, forming his own ideas. Slowly, his hands curled into fists on the arms of the dark leather chair.

''Anyway, when Daisy called Mama to say that Hugh had been in this awful car accident, and could we come—well, what else could we do?''

''Refused?'' Tucker suggested, but she shook her head.

''We'd already had...words. Daddy had already got word that he was being sent to a church in the mountains, and naturally, they expected me to go, too. But how could I?''

She looked directly at him, then, and he knew without her telling him why she hadn't wanted to go. Some of the hardness left his face.

''Hugh was in critical condition by the time we got there. He'd—it was his head and his neck that had been most injured. He wasn't even conscious most of the time, and poor Daisy was just falling apart. Mama's real good in situations like that—being a minister's wife, she's learned to cope with it, and Daisy was her friend, but they couldn't stay more than a few days, so I offered—Daisy kept insisting that Hugh had been calling for me, and—have you ever been in a hospital, Tucker?'' she asked suddenly.

Puzzled, he nodded slowly. ''Why?''

''Then you know how it is—after a few days, you lose all sight of reality. The days run together, and you don't know if it's morning or night. You forget how much time is passing, and pretty soon, nothing outside that small universe seems to matter anymore. I stayed for three weeks. Hugh rallied several times, but he couldn't do much more than look at me. He tried to talk, but—"

She took a deep breath and went on. He let her, knowing she needed it even more than he needed to hear it. "Mama and Daddy came several times—Bob Ed sent them tickets, so they felt sort of obligated. And once they were there, Hugh rallied a little bit and took hold of my hand—he kept trying to tell me something, and—oh, I don't know. It all seemed so—so reasonable at the time. Daisy insisted he was begging me to marry him, and—" She swallowed hard and plucked at a loose thread at the hem of her pale blue cotton dress. "And so I did."

Tucker was silent for a long time. When she went on silently rolling the thread around her finger, not looking up, he said, "You never worried about what you were doing to me? To us?"

"To you?" Was there a hint of guilt in her expression, or was he seeing what he wanted to see? "Tucker, I was too busy worrying about what I was doing to *me*. I didn't *want* to marry Hugh—I didn't want to marry anyone but... It never even occurred to me that you would care that much."

He swore, and she went on, her words coming more rapidly now as she tried to explain that she had known very well she was sacrificing her own happiness. "But I knew I was strong enough to bear it. Tucker, I'm a lot stronger than I look—I always have been, only you never believed me."

"Dammit, I *loved* you! Didn't you care that you were throwing away my happiness—our happiness together?"

Numbly, she shook her head. "You never said—I mean, we never really talked about our future. Together, I mean. You said you were going away and you weren't going to work for someone else all your life, and I believed you. But you never said..."

"That I planned to take you with me? Hell, I didn't think I had to say it! I was saying it every day, with every breath I took—with every damned hour I slogged over those books or beat my brains out trying to figure out how some damned piece of machinery could be made to work better! It was for *us*!''

He was up and pacing, and Hope cowered in the massive leather chair. She had slipped off her sandals and drawn her feet up beside her, and now she gripped the arms of her chair and stared up at him, shocked—and yet not really shocked—to realize that she had hurt him every bit as much as she had hurt herself.

Tucker halted in front of her, his arms hanging limply at his sides. ''What was it like, Hope?'' He had resigned himself to hearing the rest.

''It was...more or less what I expected,'' she said quietly, as if she'd been drained of all emotion. ''It lasted a lot longer than we'd thought it would, though.'' She had to pause for a moment to try to swallow the lump that had formed in her throat. ''Four years longer.''

He dropped down onto the ottoman as if he'd been poleaxed. ''Good God, you mean—was this some sort of a deathbed thing? Only he didn't die?''

''Don't say that, Tucker—it makes it sound so awful, and it wasn't that way. Poor Hugh—he couldn't speak out for himself, and we all thought we were doing the best thing— at least our parents thought so. I'm not sure I was in any condition to think.''

''Doing what you were told, like a good little girl. The thing I don't understand is, why? What did any of you have to gain from it?''

Tears had filled her eyes, and her voice was beginning to wobble.

''Oh, Tucker, don't ask me to try and make sense of anything—not now. Daisy was sick, only we didn't realize it— she couldn't stand seeing him that way, only she couldn't leave him there alone. And my parents—oh, I don't know. I guess they thought it would all be over in a few days and— and I just don't know,'' she wailed.

Tucker thought he knew, but it wouldn't help matters to bring out his suspicions—that the Outlaws had hoped to be able to provide their daughter with a nice little nest egg, and that the Phillipses, by marrying their son off, could prove to themselves that there was nothing to those old rumors that had surfaced around town from time to time about Hugh and his lack of interest in the opposite sex.

"Tucker, I'm so sorry about all of it. I'm not a wealthy widow the way you thought I was. Poor Bob Ed did all he could, and there was the insurance, but four years of round-the-clock nursing used up everything and then some. Hugh was in a body cast for so long. Part of the time he was in a coma. I couldn't handle him alone. And then when Daisy was diagnosed..."

She was openly crying, and Tucker did what he had to do. Gathering her into his arms, he crossed over to the deep, wide leather sofa and settled down, all the while murmuring words of comfort—mostly "there-there," but it seemed to do the trick, because she wrapped her arms around his neck and clung to him while she sobbed for a few minutes, and then she grew still.

For what seemed hours, they sat like that—Hope on Tucker's lap, her arms loosely around his neck, her head on his chest. Now and then a deep, shuddering sob would work its way up through her body, but other than that, neither of them made a sound.

With her soft weight pressing on him, and her scent rising warmly to his nostrils, Tucker began to experience a familiar stirring.

He tired to shift her just a bit to make it less obvious, but she refused to be shifted. "Honey—I think the ham's done, and the potatoes are probably cooked to pieces by now."

"I'm not very hungry," she murmured, her voice muffled against his chest.

"Yeah, well, I am. Starving, in fact." Only not for food, he added silently. This had been a mistake...a bi-i-ig mistake. The river had been haunted with her ghost ever since she'd left town, and now his house was going to be ruined for him, too. From now on, he'd be seeing her everywhere—smiling at his porch swing, marveling over his white kitchen floor—and now in his sitting room. "I'm going to have to throw out this furniture and start all over again," he grumbled, and she lifted her head to stare at him.

"For goodness' sake, why?"

"Because I won't be able to walk in here without remembering how you looked in that chair—how you feel on my lap when I'm sitting on my sofa—hell, I'll get hard just walking through the door!"

"Tucker!"

"What, little preacher's girl—you don't know what I'm talking about?" He held her away just enough to see her flushed face, the soft invitation of her lips.

"I suppose it's time I was leaving. It's already dark."

"Rain clouds."

"Even so..."

"Afraid?"

She met his eyes. He could see what it cost her, but she didn't flinch. "Yes. I think I'm afraid of finding out how much I lost because I didn't have the courage to stand up for myself."

He took a long time in answering her, but not once did her gaze falter. If she was trying to tell him something, he sure as hell didn't want to miss the message—or mistake it for something it wasn't. "How much courage do you have now? Enough to see if there's anything left?"

Her lips parted and she breathed audibly. He could feel the soft current against his cheek, and it nearly drove him over the edge. There was no way she could mistake what was happening to him. If she said yes...

"Yes," she whispered.

Nine

A king-size bed dominated the room. Tucker paused in the doorway, as if offering Hope one last chance to change her mind. Or come to her senses. As for his own senses, they'd been working overtime ever since she'd come back to town—ever since the first time he'd kissed her, in fact.

Hell, since before she was more than gleam in her parents' eyes, more than likely. It took more than a few days, or even a few years, to build up the head of steam he'd been generating lately.

Because he could feel her beginning to tense up, he lowered his face and nuzzled the place on the side of her neck that used to drive her wild.

That, at least, hadn't changed. She groaned and twisted in his arms, and he moved swiftly to the bed and lowered her onto the slightly crooked brown chenille spread.

Her fingers moved to the buttons at the front of her dress, and he covered her hands with his. "Let me," he whispered, "and I'll return the favor."

He remembered the first time she had worked up enough nerve to remove his shirt. He had died a thousand deaths before she had finally finished the job.

He was dying now, his hands shaking so bad he was half afraid he would tear a button off. "It drove me wild, you know—thinking about you with some other man."

The last button slipped through the small hole and he tried to drag the top of her dress over her shoulders, but she stopped him.

"There's a hook at the waist—here, I'll—"

"I'll do it. The discipline is good for my character—if it doesn't kill me first."

"Tucker, there was never anyone but you," Hope said so softly he barely caught the words. "There never could be..."

"Oh, God, sweetheart..." He ruined a good shirt and jammed the zipper on his khakis before he was able to get shed of all his clothes. Shaking like a leaf, he came down beside her, not quite touching her—afraid to do more than look. It had been too long—you'd think a man his age would have more control.

"There was never even you," she reminded him softly.

"There is now."

Reaching up, Hope clasped his face between her hands, locking her gaze with his. "Tucker, don't think about those lost years. Don't think at all."

"Think," he groaned. "Do I look like a man who's capable of thought right now? Honey, you flatter me." Sliding his hand up her wrist, he turned his face and began kissing the pale inner side of her arm and the inside of her elbow, which made her suck in her breath.

With his tongue, he traced the faint pattern of blue veins there, and then kissed his way up to the hidden hollow beneath her arm. From there he began working his way south on a different route, slowly savoring every sweet morsel of flesh. But when he felt the hard button of her nipple nudging his cheek, his control was shattered for good.

Abruptly, he rolled away, lying on his side with his back to her. The sound of his breathing in the dimly lit room was like the sound of tearing cloth.

Time—he'd promised himself he would give her time. Promised himself that if he ever got another chance with her, he wouldn't blow it by taking too much for granted. Or by rushing her.

Time. All he could think of was that they had wasted seven years!

"Tucker?" With the tentative sound of her voice came the lightest touch on his hip. He ground his teeth as he fought to control the overpowering hunger that consumed him. He'd cut the damned thing off before he would hurt her!

"Yeah—I'm sorry, honey. Give me a minute, will you?"

"If you'd rather not—" she said hesitantly, and he could feel her begin to withdraw.

"No! Sweetheart, give me a minute, will you? I don't want to rush you—the last thing I want is to hurt you in any way, but the way I feel right now, I don't think I could go easy."

He felt her warmth even before he felt her body align itself with his back, her peaked little breasts shoving into his shoulder blades, his buttocks pressed against the joint of her thighs. She was burning up down there, and when her arms slipped around his waist and she began toying with the flat curls of body hair on his belly, he grabbed her wrist and hauled her bodily over him until she was lying half on top of him.

"Would you dance on the rim of an erupting volcano?" he grated.

"I've never even seen an erupting volcano."

"Keep doing what you're doing and you're going to see one any minute now," he grated.

"I was always fascinated by geology," she murmured, her hands busy exploring. "Remember our rocks down by the river?"

"Nice kisses, you mean?"

"Gneiss and schist. You always pretended to get it wrong."

"And you always patiently spelled it out for me and showed me the difference between rocks and nice kisses."

"You probably can't even spell them yet," she teased, her breath warm and damp on his chest.

"No, but I could demonstrate a few things about hard rocks...."

Tucker thought her soft laughter would do him in, but when he felt the tip of her tongue on one of his nipples, he clenched his teeth and grabbed up fistfuls of sheets. "You gonna keep on doing that, or you gonna kill me quickly and get it over with?" The words jammed in his throat so that he could hardly get them out.

"Does it hurt? Then maybe I should do...this, instead."

"Ah, don't... stop," he moaned. "I can take just about ten seconds of that before I go stark—raving—*wild*. Ahh, Hope—sweetheart, please..." The sound hissed through his clenched teeth.

Abruptly, he lifted her so that he had access to her most sensitive places. And he knew them all. Willing himself to be patient—to wait until she had caught up with him, Tucker began caressing her, trailing his fingertips along the insides of her thighs, planting moist kisses in the hollows behind her knees. He bathed her breasts with his tongue, and then blew on the tips, watching them bead even higher.

And then he aligned his hips with hers and began a slow, rhythmic dance, brushing, touching, pressing—nestling. His hand slipped down and worked its way between their bodies, and he gently twined his fingertips in the soft pale thicket that guarded her cleft.

He was trembling with eagerness and nearly paralyzed with nervousness. "Do you remember that last summer, sweetheart?" he whispered against her lips, punctuating the words with a slow, suggestive thrust of his tongue.

"You—know I do," she gasped.

He knew. The memory was burned in him for all time—her sweet, hot innocence, her willingness. He had wanted her so desperately that he would have given his soul for what she had offered him. But not hers. And knowing her beliefs—knowing she was incapable of lying, and that her parents would know, and they would either send her away or force her to marry him before he could take care of her, thus ruining all his plans for their future, he had touched her, kissed her, and told her they would wait.

And for seven years, they had waited.

"Please—oh, please, Tucker," she whimpered. She was writhing helplessly as his fingers continued to caress her, to touch her in that special way that brought a wild flush to her cheeks.

"Are you sure?" Eyes gleaming like dark coals, he cupped her soft mound in his hand, stroking slowly. She was damp with the dew of desire, and he knew that she was ready for him.

"Tuck-errrr," she groaned, and sliding her hands down to the creases of his thighs, she brought them inward, combing her thumbs through the short dense hair that cradled his manhood.

Tucker nearly went through the roof. When he felt her small hot hands close around him, he was shaken by a hard shudder. "No, I can't—ahhhh—right there, sweetheart. Yes-s-s-ss . . ." And then, reluctantly, "No—no more!"

He turned away briefly, and she curled around his backside while he unrolled protection. His hands were shaking almost too much to do the job.

Then, positioning her thighs, he knelt between them. "I'll take it slow," he promised, wondering how much a man could stand and keep his sanity.

He was never given the chance to find out. Hope slipped her legs around his hips and lifted her own, and with a muffled cry, he slipped inside her.

She was so tight, so . . . Ah, jeez, no! His heart was pounding until it felt like the surf crashing over his head. Desperately, he tried to slow the onslaught, but it was no use. She was holding him, drawing him into the vortex, and he followed her willingly. Head pressed into the pillow, she stared directly into his eyes, and Tucker felt himself whirling into the final spiral that had begun even before he had entered her.

As she pulsated tightly around him, he rode harder, faster, knowing that there was no stopping short of the final destination. "Come on, love," he urged. "Come *onnnn*!" Burying his face in her throat, he hurtled that last endless step on the infinite journey into oblivion.

She was gone when he opened his eyes again. Gone! Tucker couldn't believe it. He rolled out of bed, shot a scowling look at the glow-in-the-dark face of his alarm clock and saw that it was barely ten o'clock.

Taking time only to step into a pair of jeans and ram the zipper partway up, he raced through the house, glancing into each room as he passed it. The journey took less than a minute.

She was nowhere to be found. He'd checked everywhere. But unless she'd taken his car keys from his pocket and borrowed his car, she couldn't have gotten far.

The thought of her walking home alone at night brought a cold sweat to his brow. As shabby as it was, Shacktown was no high crime district. Even so, she could run into a drunk staggering home from Greasy's, or one of the tough kids who hung out at J.J.'s.... There was a slight risk that she could stumble across a drug deal, and knowing Hope, she'd probably try to interfere—especially if kids were involved.

Swearing under his breath, Tucker stalked into the kitchen again and poured himself a glass of milk. To his amazement, she had turned off his slow cooker before she'd left.

Now what kind of woman would get up out of bed after having made love for the first time in her life—and he knew damned well it *had* been her first time—and turn off a slow cooker?

Tucker was puzzled. Not only that, he was worried. And when he got worried, as often as not, he got angry.

Damn her silky little hide, where did she get off walking out on him a second time? He'd forgiven her for the first time—hell, he could even understand it in a crazy sort of way. Not one woman in ten thousand would have done what she'd done, but that was Hope. She'd been brainwashed for so long that when it came to looking out for her own interests, she didn't have a clue.

She needed him. Always had, always would. He could picture her now, eighty years old and still letting people take advantage of her good nature . . .

Dammit, she *needed* him!

Morosely, Tucker glared at the half-finished glass of milk. He'd fallen asleep with Hope's head tucked up under his chin and his own head full of half-formed plans. She'd sprawled over him like a silk blanket, and as hot as it was, all he could think about was spending the next hundred or so years with her, holding her in his arms every night, coming home after work to see what she'd done with herself all day—what the kids had been up to.

They'd have good kids. She'd be a terrific mother. He would teach his boys the satisfaction of working—of building things with their own hands, but his daughter . . . ah, his daughter would be every bit as protected and cherished as her mother had been. She'd be his own little princess, just like her mother was.

Groaning, Tucker buried his face in his hands. She was gone, dammit, and he was sitting here like a slug of cup-grease when he should be out looking for her.

Abruptly, he got up from the table and strode silently into the parlor. His keys should be on the table where he always left them, unless she'd borrowed his car.

But if she'd driven herself home, she had done it wearing no more than her underpants and his shirt, because the rest of her things were still scattered all over his bedroom.

He switched on a harsh overhead light in the living room and swore softly. The place was already haunted. He could still smell the faint elusive fragrance that always seemed to cling to her skin and her hair. Closing his eyes, he could almost hear her voice....

His eyes snapped open again. He *had* heard her voice! Either that or he was further around the bend than he'd thought.

"Hope?"

"Out here."

He went charging through the front door with no regard at all for any sleeping neighbors. The screen door slammed loudly behind him as he confronted the shadowy figure curled up in one corner of his front porch swing.

The chain squeaked. Tucker drew a deep, steadying breath and willed himself to rev down. "What are you doing out here?" he asked as he sat down beside her, being careful not to touch her.

"I needed to think."

"Yeah, well...okay." Why not? He'd already done his thinking. He'd had seven years to think. All he'd had to do when she'd come back to town was haul out his old dreams and dust them off. Some things didn't require a whole lot of planning.

"Tucker, I think we need to talk."

He thought hard and fast. This was probably a good time for some pretty words, only he'd never been much good with pretty words. Intentions, now—that was another matter. He figured it was long past time that he let her in on his intentions. "Yeah, well—what I was thinking is that George Harrington called last week to tell me I've been invited to join the Chamber of Commerce, which is supposed to be some kind of big deal, I think.

"He also happened to mention that there were some nice houses going up west of town. Two- and three-acre lots, plenty of trees—he said his bank was financing most of them, and if I was interested..."

"Houses? But you already have a home."

Unexpectedly, Tucker felt a rush of heat sting his face and was glad of the darkness. "Oh, this place—it's okay, but

I've been thinking about maybe finding something nicer. You know—with plenty of room for a garden and a wading pool for the kids and that kind of thing. You like apples? We could have our own fruit trees. And you'd be nearer to all your friends, so—''

"What friends?" Hope interrupted. Her voice sounded kind of tight, and Tucker, who had absently set the swing in motion, grew still again.

"Gabby's place still wouldn't be all that far, and there's bound to be people you used to know, people from your dad's church. But if you don't like the western part of town, we could look somewhere else. Anywhere you want to live is okay by me.''

"Anywhere?"

"Sure—we'd want it to be safe and nice for the kids and all, but I'd be willing to leave the final choice pretty much up to you.''

Tucker waited for a response, and then he waited some more. She was too quiet. He began to get nervous. And when he got nervous, he either said what was on his mind flat out and let the chips fly, or he clammed up completely. "Okay, you want the truth? I'm not sure I could stomach living on the Ridge, but if that's what you want, I'm willing to give it a try. I reckon I can afford it.''

"You've got it all planned, haven't you?"

Suddenly, Tucker knew how it felt it to be walking through a mine field. "No, not completely. I told you, wherever you want to live is just fine with me, as long as it's, um...suitable.''

"Oh? And you're the one to say whether it's suitable or not?"

"Now, honey, you know you wouldn't want to—"

"Dammit, Tucker, you don't even know what you're doing to me, do you?''

"I'm only trying to make you see reason. If you won't take care of yourself, someone's got to—"

"Who appointed you lord mayor of my life?"

Completely out of his depth, Tucker grasped for the only reality he could think of. "You came back to me. I know you love me—if you didn't, you'd never have made love with me. And God knows, if there's one thing I learned how to do while you were gone, it was how to love you even more than I did before. If you've got some problem with that, I reckon we'll just have to work it out." His features had taken on a harsh, angular look. He attempted a smile that didn't quite come off. "Honey, that's my specialty—working out problems."

"Did it ever occur to you that I'm not a piece of machinery?" she asked quietly, and he didn't know quite how to respond to that.

Her sigh cut through him like a sharp blade. He could feel her begin to withdraw, feel it just as surely as if she had put on her dress and shoes and walked out on him.

She was wearing the shirt he'd taken off—the one he'd practically ripped the sleeve out of trying to remove. That was a good sign, wasn't it? "Look, honey, why don't we talk about this tomorrow? Isn't it enough that we're together again, and we still love each other as much as ever? More, in fact."

"How do you know that?"

That shook him. He stared at her, trying to make out the expression on her face. "You trying to tell me you don't love me now? No way, honey. I'm not buying it. You're not the kind of woman to go to bed with a man she doesn't love— you never will be."

"How do you know what kind of woman I am, Tucker? Did you ever once offer me the chance to show you?" And before he could answer that, she rushed on to say, "You're just like my parents! They think I'm some sort of an extension of them—they think and I react. They say jump and up I go. And you're doing the same thing. You always did, only seven years ago—ten years ago—I needed that! I needed someone like you to prove to me that the world wouldn't come to an end if I disobeyed my parents."

Tucker went cold. "Someone like me?"

"Well—you, then. All right, I needed you."

"And you still do."

"No, dammit, I don't! I might *want* you, but that's not the same. And if you can't see the difference, then I don't see where we have any chance for a future, do you?"

"You're asking the wrong man that question, honey." His laughter fell like a bitter rain on the soft night air.

"Tucker, can we talk about this later? I really do need to get home now. I have to get up extra early because Mrs. Wooten wants to bring Bobbi and Traci in at seven instead of eight-thirty tomorrow—she has to go to Durham because her sister's in the hospital there."

"Oh, hell, yes, we don't want to inconvenience Mrs. Wooten!" He forced himself to calm down. Harsh words weren't going to help matters. "You want to get dressed first, go ahead. I'll be in in a few minutes."

It was clam-up time. He may not have a degree in psychology—or anything else, for that matter—but it didn't take a college education to know when it was time to stop beating his head against a brick wall.

Billy was getting to be a problem. Hope knew she should do something, but she didn't know how to discourage the boy without hurting his feelings.

"Tell him Cheri's got the hots for him," Gabby suggested. Cheri, a junior high student, was one of the new part-time volunteers.

"Then he'd get his feelings hurt when she turned him down. Cheri's got a crush on Hog Jemison."

"J.J.'s boy? Girl's got great taste. That boy's got buns to die for. You ought to see him leaning over one of his daddy's billiard tables in a pair of tight jeans."

"When did you ever see the inside of J.J.'s?"

"While you were in Sunday School, probably." Gabby chuckled as she lined up her freshly washed espadrilles on the balcony rail. "Honey, it's not really a den of iniquity. My brother used to go by and collect cans for the recycler, and when I was with him, J.J. would give me a piece of chalk so I could draw on the sidewalk. That was before Hog was even born, I reckon."

"Yes, well . . . buns or no, he's at least ten years younger than you are, so I'd watch my step if I were you. Mr. Harrington thinks you're such a serious minded business woman, it'd be a darn shame if he ever learned the truth."

Shoes washed and set out to dry, Gabby propped her elbows on the rail and gazed out over the parking lot to the slice of river that glinted between units one and three. "What time'd you get in last night?" she asked casually.

"Not too late."

"It was after eleven."

"If you knew, why'd you ask?" Hope had been applying a coat of clear polish to her nails to remind her not to chew on them. She only did it when she was deeply troubled. So far she'd mowed down both thumbnails and was halfway across her left hand.

"You were out with Tucker, weren't you?"

"My car wouldn't start. He gave me a lift."

"A lift onto what—his bed?"

Hope looked up, her face flaming. "I wish you wouldn't say things like that! You made me mess up a fingernail."

"Better than messing up your life. Are you moving in with him? If you are, can I buy your bed? My sister wants to come to town and try to find a job."

"You can have my bed if you want it so much," said Hope stiffly. After a sleepless night spent wondering if she'd thrown away her one chance of happiness, the last thing she needed was rejection from her best friend. "I'll look for another place today."

"Hey, don't get your back up, I was only suggesting—"

"I am not moving in with Tucker! If you must know, he asked me to marry him . . . I think."

Gabby sent her speculative look. "You *think*? Honey, if you're that naïve, you don't deserve a man like Tucker Owen."

"I am not naïve. He wants to marry me. At least he was talking about a house in that new subdivision west of town, with a garden and a wading pool. That hardly sounds like a—a liaison to me."

"A liaison. Hmm. Is that what you Ridgebacks call it? In my neck of the woods, we call it—"

"I *know* what you call it, darn it! Gabby, am I being paranoid?"

"I wouldn't know. Has Tucker been acting like a boogeyman?"

"You know how it was with my parents? I couldn't date until I was fifteen, and then I could only date Hugh because they didn't want me to get mixed up with a—a 'rough element.'"

"Meaning Tucker."

"Probably. But it wasn't just that. Mama chose my clothes for me, even when I tried to tell her none of the girls wore frilly blouses and flowered dresses to school—and Daddy insisted that I stay home and take classes at the community college when I wanted to go to State and study geology."

"Nice little girls don't get their mitts grimy mucking around in the dirty old ground, huh?"

"Something like that. Daddy was more worried about field trips with mixed groups all sleeping in tents and nobody chaperoning."

"Your papa must've been a real doozy in his day. They say the wildest ones make the strictest parents."

"Gabby, for goodness' sake," Hope exclaimed. "Daddy's a minister!"

"So? He and your mama figured out how to have you, didn't they? Or did someone leave you in the collection plate one Sunday morning?"

"Look, if you're going to listen, then stop interrupting with crude remarks about things that don't concern you."

Gabby's dark eyebrows shot up like a pair of pup tents. "Well, pardon *me*."

"Oh, I'm sorry. I didn't mean that—you know I didn't, only I'm so mixed up. I couldn't sleep last night for worrying, and then Billy followed me around all day, and when he wasn't actually following me, he was—sort of staring. You know, sort of moonstruck? And then the Coleridge twins threw up and I'm afraid they might be coming down with something which means—"

"I can guess what it means. Now get on with the good stuff—how'd Tucker ask you? Did he give you a ring?"

"Actually, he didn't really ask me. He just started talking about the house, and the Chamber of Commerce, and apple trees and wading pools, and I know just as well as I know my own name that he expects me to quit work and—and play lady all day long!"

Gabby gave a sputter of laughter. "So? A lot of women wouldn't find that too hard to take."

"Gabby, if I marry Tucker, it'll be just exactly like it was living with Mama and Daddy."

"With a few interesting variations," Gabby said suggestively.

"You know what I mean. He won't want me to work, he won't want me to even visit over in Shacktown—he'll expect me to sit on a silk cushion and sew a fine seam . . . or whatever."

"And you'll only get to watch the Disney Channel on TV, because you might be corrupted if you were to tune into *Oprah* or *Dallas*—or heaven forbid, the network news."

Against her will, Hope had to laugh. "I know, it sounds awful. Like I'm some poor weakling who wouldn't say boo to a goose."

"I don't know about booing any geese, but it seems to me you did a pretty good job of going after what you wanted before you ever got railroaded into marrying Hugh Phillips. I mean, we both know you and Tucker didn't spend all your time helping each other with your homework."

After a long moment of staring out into space, Hope said quietly, "I love him so much. I honestly think I would die for him, but the thing is, I don't know if I can give up my life for him. Does that make any kind of sense at all?"

Ten

———

It's another headache, isn't it? Tucker, if you don't go get your eyes examined, I'm going to get your doggone head examined," Evelyn snapped. "I thought you'd be dancing on top of your desk."

"I do not have a headache, and I am thrilled silly—tickled pink," Tucker snarled. "Now, are you satisfied?"

"Well, considering how hard you worked to get it, I thought you'd at least declare a half-day holiday."

"You wanna leave? Take off! My blessings on you."

Tucker swiveled his chair around and lifted his moccasined feet to the windowsill. He tilted back until the chair struck his desk, which was littered with papers and rough schematic drawings. On top of the stack was a letter from a community-development specialist with the council of governments that announced the awarding of a six-hundred-thousand-dollar federal grant for the renovation of some thirty-seven substandard houses in the eastern section of Princetown, between the Tar River and Chinaberry Street.

With a sigh that was completely out of character, Tucker spun his chair around and managed a half-hearted smile for the woman who had put up with his rotten disposition and his crazy working habits since the first day he had opened the doors of Owen Automotive.

"Look, I'm really sorry, Evelyn. I know you sweated this one out every step of the way, but—"

"You did the sweating, Tucker. All I did was put it in letter form."

"We both know who mapped a trail through several hundred miles of bureaucratic jungle. Thanks, Evvie. It wouldn't have happened without you."

"Sure it would. They don't call you Take-Charge Tucker for nothing. Only thing is, if you hadn't had me to keep you in control you probably would've ended up in jail on a charge of first-degree skull-cracking."

He grinned at that. They both knew there was more than a little truth in it. Tucker had been called a lot of things in his life, Take-Charge Tucker being among the milder. He did have a tendency to take charge. If he'd had to wait on the civic conscience of Princetown's political clique to get the ball rolling, Shacktown would've disintegrated into a small heap of tin, tar paper and termites. It hadn't taken him long to learn that business, River Ridge-style, was conducted over drinks or on a golf course—or both.

Which was why he'd gone first to Raleigh and then to Washington and rattled a few cages himself. Since his drinking was limited to a single beer or a glass of wine, and he had neither the time nor the inclination to learn to play golf, he had taken a more direct route.

"Okay, okay, we still have a business to run, woman. Get Paxton on the line for me, and have that file handy. Oh, and call air freight. See if you can chase down those valve train components. They were supposed to be on a 4:20 flight out of Detroit yesterday."

"Right. And Tucker—Mr. Proctor called about Wanda Coe. He wants to talk to you again before he interviews her, and I told him you'd get back to him within fifteen minutes. That was fourteen minutes ago."

Tucker muttered something faintly derogatory about self-winding secretaries and Evelyn closed the door softly behind her. She was smiling. "Trouble in paradise," she sang softly to the tune of "April in Paris."

It was nearly one o'clock before Tucker was able to get away from his office. He had enough ham in the refrigerator to keep him in sandwiches for a week, but he didn't feel like going home to eat. Or to sleep, or anything else.

He'd been right about one thing—it had been a mistake to take her home with him. The first thing on his mind when he'd opened his eyes after a sleepless night was Hope. She had used his pillow. She had used his towel. He fancied he could smell her scent on everything he touched.

She'd been the one to turn off the slow cooker under the ham he couldn't bring himself to eat. She'd sat at his kitchen table, she'd sat in his chair—she'd swung in his swing and as good as told him she didn't love him enough to marry him.

Angrily, he downshifted and spun out of the parking lot with all the finesse of a green kid taking his first turn under the wheel. He would go to Lin Tuan's for lunch. And if that happened to take him directly past the community center, then what the hell? He had as much right to be there as she did. He wasn't going to see her; he just wanted to be sure the place was being properly taken care of, and that all the departments had everything they needed and that . . .

Oh, hell.

She was out on the playground, bending over a bald-headed kid about two feet long who was bawling his eyes out. Within seconds, she had him grinning again, bouncing him on her hip and tapping his nose lightly with her forefinger.

Tucker knew a pang of envy for the kid. He was about to pull away without stopping when she looked directly at him. Never one to back down from a challenge, he shut off the engine and opened the door. But he took his own sweet time getting out, levering one long leg out at a time while she continued to stare at him. By the time he let himself in the gate, she had lowered the child to the ground, where he'd scampered off again. But she hadn't moved away.

"Hi," he greeted coolly. "Just thought I'd check around inside, see if everything's under control. Looks like you've got it ticking over pretty smoothly out here."

He nodded and would have passed her by—or died trying—when she called him back.

"Tucker... do you have a minute?"

He did his damndest to keep the excitement and satisfaction he felt from showing on his face, but he had a hunch he might be lit up like a neon sign. He'd known she would come around sooner or later. No way could the Hope he knew have made love to him that way unless she was still crazy about him. A man could sense that sort of thing, and for all his shortcomings in other areas, Tucker knew his instincts where Hope Outlaw was concerned were first-rate.

He watched while she delegated one of the high school girls to take over for her, and then she hurried over to where he was leaning against the cool brick wall. There was no way on God's green earth he could keep the smile off his face when she gazed up at him with that worried little pucker between her silky brown eyebrows.

"'Afternoon, Miss Hope," he said softly.

"Oh. Good afternoon." The frown deepened and she flushed, making her hair look even lighter where she'd pulled it away from her face. Was he imagining it, or was there a special sort of glow about her today?

No... there'd always been that glow about her, he concluded. But it was specially noticeable after they'd made love. Tucker felt himself swelling with pride. Skittish or not, she was still his woman—which made him one hell of a man! "Say, do you reckon you could get away for a—" he began when she interrupted him.

"Tucker, I need to talk to you about Billy."

His jaw dropped. "Billy?"

"Billy Coe. I understand he's a special friend of yours?"

Tucker frowned. "Yeah. So? Is he making a nuisance of himself? I'll keep him out of your hair from now on, Hope—don't give it another thought."

"But you can't just order him to stay away. Tucker, he's a really sweet boy, but I think—that is, I'm afraid—well, he seems to have some idea that I . . ."

"He's in love with you."

Now she looked everywhere but at his face, her hands twisting in front of her. "He's only fourteen."

"And a half. I was fourteen when I first met you, remember?"

"That was different."

"Was it?"

"Oh, for goodness' sake, we're talking about a child and an adult!"

"You were a child."

"And you were, too."

His look was one of acceptance, holding neither pain nor sadness. "At fourteen-and-a-half, I was no child. Neither is Billy in a lot of ways. Some kids grow up too fast."

Hope nibbled on her bottom lip, and Tucker seemed unable to drag his gaze away from the sight of her small white teeth tormenting the pink morsel of flesh. "Has he been stepping out of line?"

"No, not really. He's just—always there. And he looks at me a lot."

A quizzical smile shifted the angular planes of Tucker's features as he said, "Honey, I hate to be the one to break the news, but unless you take to going around with a tote sack over your head, there's no way you're going to keep people from looking." His eyes strayed down over her body, taking in the pink-and-white striped sleeveless cotton, the red braided belt that spanned her diminutive waist, and the length of tanned and shapely legs that ended in a pair of white sandals, size six and a half, narrow. "In fact, better make that a shower curtain instead of a paper bag."

Hope stared out at the children swarming over the jungle gym and the sandpile for several moments, while Tucker tried to think of a subtle way to bring up what had happened the night before. But before he could speak, she turned to him and said, "Tucker, about last night . . ."

He swallowed hard and said, "Um—what about it?"

"I don't know any way to put this except to say right out how I feel." Acorn-brown eyes pleaded with him to understand, and Tucker felt a prickle of uneasiness between his shoulder blades.

I don't want to hear this. If she's going to say what I think she's going to say, then please, God—let it start snowing first. Let a tree blow over—send down anything at all, but just don't let her say she doesn't want to see me any more.

"Go ahead—I can take it."

A small whirlwind in red overalls plowed to a stop and yanked on Hope's skirt. "Miss Hope, Miss Hope—Cathy's been feeding rocks to Jeffy and I can't make him spit 'em out."

Thank you, God. It was a little drastic, but then, kids eat rocks all the time. Roughage is supposed to be healthy, right?

While Hope was upending the rock eater, Tucker made his escape, having decided that he wasn't yet ready to listen to her explain why she didn't want him in her life anymore.

"Gabby, he brought me flowers! What am I going to do?" Hope stared in dismay at the arrangement of short-stemmed zinnias and top-heavy hydrangeas in a mason jar that had magically appeared on her desk.

"You wanted roses? So trash 'em if it'll make you feel better."

"That's not the point and you know it! I can't encourage him to keep bringing me things. Yesterday it was those tomatoes. Honestly, it's getting so I almost hate to come to work. I spoke to Tucker, but—"

"But?" Gabby, having left her door open to listen out for the nappers while Hope took the older children out to play, had slipped off her shoes and gotten herself a soft drink from the machine in the hall.

"But we got interrupted, and he had to leave. Cathy gave Jeff Abernathy rocks and told him they were candy, and I got bitten trying to take them away from him. It's bad enough that I bite my own nails without getting help from a two-year-old."

"They were awfully good tomatoes—must've been Early Girls. Are you sure—?"

"Gabby!"

"Okay, okay—I have an idea that just might work. Tucker would have to cooperate, though."

"I don't know when I'll see him again," Hope said wistfully. Gabby promptly handed her the phone, but she shook her head. "I couldn't."

"Sure you could. I'll even dial for you."

"Gabby, you don't understand—the way things were between us—well, I'm not even sure if he wants to see me again."

"No, and I'm not sure the sun's gonna come up again tomorrow, but I'd be willing to lay odds on it. Call him, you dunce! If you don't, I will. Daddy's tomatoes will be coming in in a week or so, and besides, once Billy cleans his mama out of flowers, there's no telling what he'll be dragging in here. May as well straighten the poor kid out before he starts hauling in skateboard loads of—"

"Oh, for pity sake, give me the phone!" Hope dialed Tucker's office and let it ring a dozen times. Evidently, both he and his secretary were out. "Maybe I'll try later," she said with an air of reprieve. "But even if I get him, I won't know what to say. What is this plan of yours, anyway?"

Gabby noisily drained the last of her drink and crushed the can in one hand. "Comes from milking goats. Betcha you can't do that," she crowed.

"Why would I ever want to, for pity sake? Gabby, do you suppose Tucker would—"

"Whoa! Let's handle Operation Billy first, okay? Then you two lovebirds can get back to arguing over who's going to live where. You remember when I told you to let Billy think Cheri was interested in him?"

Puzzled, Hope nodded.

"Well, with a minor twist, the same thing can still work. All we have to do is let him know that you belong to Tucker, right?"

"But that would be cruel." Hope went on counting out cookies, napkins and small paper cups.

"Oh, I dunno—he might have a humungous crush on you, but he downright idolizes Tucker, so maybe he'll be happy to make the sacrifice. Might work."

"I don't know—it still sounds pretty risky. Besides, what makes you think Tucker would go along with it?"

"Are you kidding? Anyhow, what else can you do? Wait until Billy's old enough and marry him to put him out of his misery?"

"Oh, for goodness' sake, why can't I just talk to him?"

"Okay, I'll bite—why can't you just talk to him?"

Hope's shoulders slumped. She sighed, staring out at the playground, where Cheri had lined up all fourteen children for the march inside. "Time for washup, cookies and juice. And I can't talk to him because I don't know what to say. This has never happened to me before. I don't want to hurt his feelings, but somehow I've got to make him understand that . . . that . . ."

"That he's a kid and you're a woman, and never the twain shall meet," Gabby finished for her.

"Words to that effect, at least. Okay, man your battle stations, here they come, and the Snyder baby is waking up already." She began to direct the children. "Here, Cathy, you go in and wash your hands first. Tommy, we play with our indoors toys inside. Leave the dump truck on the deck and then brush the sand off your hands."

And in an undertone to Gabby, "I've got to come in tonight and reorganize this place. I thought I'd try putting the chairs and tables—Betsy, we'll take out the crayons and drawing papers *after* we have our refreshments."

* * *

Tucker held off calling until just after dark. He'd been sitting in his kitchen trying to make a priority list of houses to be renovated, starting with Miss Polly's. Hers was larger than some of the others, but according to his contractor friend, it was in worse shape.

Finally he threw down his pencil and reached for the phone. "Gabby, is Hope there? This is Tucker."

He listened for a moment and then frowned. And then he chuckled. "Yeah, well...good luck to you.... Thanks. See you later."

So-ooo, that was an interesting new development. It seemed that Gabby was going out to dinner with one John Quincy Marshall III, whom she'd met when he'd stopped by to see Hope the night before.

If Gabby was thrilled at the way things had turned out, Tucker was positively purring. He hadn't seriously considered JQM3 as competition—all the same, there was this niggling feeling in the back of his mind that the smooth bastard with his fancy white jacket and his shiny white loafers was much more Hope's type than Tucker would ever be.

He stood, his rather stern face split in a wide grin, and stepped into his moccasins. If Hope had to work late rearranging furniture, she could do with a little strong-armed help. Granted, the furniture in question was scaled for Lilliputians, she *still* needed his help. Always had—always would. What's more, he was going to make damned sure she realized it.

Hope had brought Gabby's portable radio to work by, and now she was shoving chairs and tables across the hardwood floor to the tune of the "Washington Post March." It was surprising how a rousing march could lift a woman's spirits. Plopping a chair on the far left side of the room, she executed a smart about-face and barged into Tucker, who was grinning from ear to ear.

"At ease, soldier," he said with a chuckle that brought color to her face.

"Dis-*missed*," she barked right back, wishing her heart didn't leap quite so high at the sight of him.

"Thought you could use a hand. What's going on around here?"

Stepping away from his too large, too compelling presence, Hope made an effort to compose himself. It wasn't easy when she'd been caught playing silly games, dressed in a pair of ancient shorts and a shirt that had belonged to Hugh. For comfort, she had tied the shirt in a knot at her midriff. "The—ah, I'm moving," she said inanely.

"Out?"

"Just over." He was too darned beautiful for a man, granite jaw, slatey eyes and crooked nose notwithstanding. "It took exactly three days for the kids to learn how to stack furniture to get into the top cabinet."

"While you were watching?"

She had no intention of incriminating her teenage helpers. All three had learned very quickly that you don't dare turn your back on a child for a single moment. "They're pretty speedy."

Tucker had a feeling they were talking on more than one level. He could have sworn her face hadn't been quite so pink, nor her eyes so bright, when he'd come into the room. It had never been his intention to sneak up on her, but with his soft-soled moccasins, he'd been no match for the crashing cymbals and the blaring trumpets.

"I just thought I'd stop by—I saw the lights on." Her eyes met his with all the candor he remembered so well, compelling him to level with her, "Actually, I came here looking for you. I called your place first, and Gabby told me where you were. We need to talk, Hope."

"About Billy?"

"About us." *About you and me and the fact that I'm so damned crazy in love with you I can't think straight. About the fact that all in the world I want is to take care of you and love you for the rest of our natural born days, but I don't seem to be able to get my message across too well.*

Hope turned away and toyed with a colorful poster depicting an apple with arms and legs and a glass of milk in its hand. "About us? I thought we'd already covered that subject."

"You thought I was going to let it go at that? Honey, there's something bugging you, and I can't for the life of me figure out what it is. I've offered to do anything you want, to buy us a house wherever you want it, and if we can't find one that suits you, I'll build whatever you want, wherever you want it. All I know is I can't handle much more of this uncertainty. I've got to *do* something!"

"*You've* got to do something. What about what *I* want to do?"

Tucker had a fleeting sensation of seeing his life pass before his eyes. "All you have to do is tell me," he said quietly. *As long as you don't tell me to get the hell out of your life.* "Haven't I said I'd do anything you wanted? All you have to do is ask."

"No, you've said you're willing to build me whatever kind of house I want, as long as it's where you think it should be and it fits in with your idea of what's right for me."

His eyes narrowed, and when she didn't immediately go on, he said, "So? You got a problem with that?"

"You're damned right I've got a problem with that! Tucker, don't you see what you're doing to me? To us?"

He didn't know her in this mood...although, come to think of it, there was something familiar about the glint in her eyes. It reminded him of all those times when she had wanted to defy her parents and lacked the nerve, and he'd had to talk sense into her, make her see that they'd only been trying to do what they considered best for her.

"So what is it you think I'm trying to do to you?" he asked finally. "Just what is it that you really want from me?"

"All I want," she said firmly, "is to move into your house on the corner of Bias and Pine and work at the center during the day and take courses at the community center at night."

He could feel his blood pressure skyrocketing as arguments began formulating themselves in his head.

"And if you still want to—to marry me," she went on in a quietly determined voice, "then I'd like that just fine, because I've never loved anyone but you. If you don't want to marry me, I'll still live with you." She swallowed hard, and her eyes skittered sideways. "That is, if you want me to."

Tucker groaned. How did a guy fight something like this?

He tried reasoning. "Sweetheart, there's nothing I want more than to marry you—I've loved you ever since the very first time you kissed me, with your mouth all puckered up and your eyes squinched up tight." How the devil could he make her understand? "But don't you see? It's *because* I love you so damned much that I refuse to drag you down to my level. I've accomplished a lot in the past eight or ten years, honey, and it's all on account of you. I had to know I could take care of you the way you deserved, and—"

She started to interrupt, but he held up a restraining hand. "No, let me finish. You've got to understand, Hope—I'm not about to allow you to lower your standards on my account. Your old man would have my scalp, and I wouldn't blame him."

He had failed to notice the set of her jaw, the thinning line of her lips and the militant squaring of her delicate shoulders. "Are you quite done?" she asked softly, and he swallowed hard and nodded.

"Then let me just say this. You asked me what I wanted. You *did* ask me, didn't you? I told you exactly what I wanted. If you're not interested, all you have to do is say so."

Lord, you don't have to let some kid eat rocks again, but how about a nice bolt of lightning? You gotta get me out of this before I blow it.

"Four rooms, Hope. Hell, we wouldn't even have room for your folks to visit once we started having kids." He ventured a smile, hoping to lighten the tension. "Hey...you do want kids, don't you?"

"Of course I do. I've always loved children."

"Me, too. Only not too many, and not right away, because we'd want to have some time for just us." *Time for me to build you the finest palace any princess ever had, one you won't be ashamed to bring your parents to.*

"Oh, Tucker, I only want us to be together, always. That's all I've ever wanted."

"I know, I know, darlin'." A slow smile spreading over his face, he gathered her into his arms and she buried her face in the hollow of his chest. Maybe it wasn't a fair way to fight, but dammit, he knew what was best for her. He always had.

"I knew you'd understand once I explained," she whispered, and he murmured something unintelligible while his fingers curved into the hollow of her spine below the shirt and above her shorts. Her skin was warm and silken, and he lost all hope of reason within seconds. All he could think of was the feel of her, all fragile bones and soft warm flesh—the smell of her, like honeysuckle and nectarines and sunshine—and the taste of her.

Oh God—the taste of her!

Shuddering with desire, Tucker brought one hand around between them to caress the soft swell of her breast. With any encouragement at all, he would undress her and lay her down on one of those pint-size tables and take her right here in the middle of the blocks and the toy trucks and the Raggedy Ann dolls.

"I never knew march music could be so—"

"So what?" he muttered, cradling her hips in the palm of one hand to lift her closer to his own aching need. As she moved against him, he felt the air leave his lungs and struggled to draw in another breath. "God, sweetheart, don't move—I'm burning a short fuse."

"It's a lovely fuse," she teased, nuzzling the opening of his khaki shirt, where the dark hair tufted against his chest. "Tucker, why were you so—so difficult when I first came back to town?"

It took him a moment to make out what she was getting at. "Difficult? Yeah, I guess that's one way of putting it.

Honey, you still don't know what it did to me, do you? You going off like that and growing up on me, and me not having any part in it. That hurt, love—I hope you don't ever know a hurt like that.''

Her arms tightened around his waist, and she closed her eyes. ''Don't you think I hurt just as much? Every day of my life—every hour while I was away from you—Tucker, you were always there with me. I don't think I could have gotten through it without you in my heart. I kept remembering how strong you were—and how good. And how you used to be so patient with me when you were trying to explain why my parents wouldn't let me do some of the things I wanted to do, and all the while, I was dying to make love with you.''

''I know, sweet—if they'd ever had any idea how close we came to it, I'd have been tarred and feathered, and you'd have ended up in a convent somewhere in the North Pole.''

She laughed softly, the sound reverberating along his spine with telling results. ''I don't think the Baptists have convents, and I'm pretty sure there aren't any at the North Pole, but I suppose Daddy would've found the nearest thing to it.''

Tucker stood with his hips propped against a windowsill, his arms around the slender woman in the yellow shorts and the white cotton shirt. Between kisses, he would whisper to her, and she would smile and murmur something to him, and then they would kiss again.

Neither of them were aware of the boy who watched from the hallway, his eyes burning with hurt anger and his fists curling helplessly at his sides.

Eleven

―――――

Tucker, I can't just walk out and leave this mess,'' Hope protested, laughing.

"You can come in early and straighten up the chairs and tables. I'll come do it for you.'' Tucker swung her up in his arms and she clutched at his shoulders. "I want you so bad I'm aching, love—and I don't think there's a single bed in this place, do you?''

"Or even a double one,'' she teased, and he growled playfully.

Still holding her, Tucker crossed to the inside door that opened onto the hallway. "I should've taken care of locking up and switching off the lights before my arms got full of woman.'' He lifted a knee and braced it against the wall in order to support her weight. By this time, they were both laughing helplessly.

"You could always let me go,'' she suggested.

Fumbling with the lock, Tucker grunted a small oath. "Oh, no, honey—not on your life. You're not getting away from me that easy, not..." He fell silent. "Did you hear something?" he asked quietly.

"Besides my own heartbeat?"

He waited a moment, and then he shook his head. "Must be my imagination. I don't see any lights in any of the offices. Have you seen anyone else around here tonight?"

Wordlessly, Hope shook her head. A sudden chill lifted goose bumps on her arms. "But I didn't really look. The only time I left the day-care area was when I went to get a broom and dustpan from the cleaning closet. The door was stuck—I couldn't open it, but I didn't see anyone around."

After a moment's pause, Tucker locked the door and turned off the lights. "This is no place for you. I've told you over and over, and—"

"Tucker," Hope said warningly, and he bit off what he'd been going to say.

"Come on, I'm taking you home," he growled.

Neither of them spoke on the short drive. Sooner or later they were going to have to come to terms with Tucker's take-charge attitude, but not now. Not tonight.

"By the way, I straightened Billy out—he won't have so much time to get into trouble from now on," he said casually as he turned onto his own street. When they'd left the center, Hope had been afraid he was going to take her to her apartment.

"You got him a job? Tucker, he's not really old enough, is he?"

"I got his mama a job in the plant section at Proctor's Hardware, with the understanding that Billy could do odd jobs to help out. The thing is, Wanda can't read. She's a whiz when it comes to plants—that woman could make a telephone pole sprout leaves—but she needs Billy around to do her reading for her."

"Did you think of hiring her out to the power company? They could grow their own," Hope said dryly, and Tucker reached over and tugged playfully on her left ear. She was sitting as close to him as she could possibly manage, and when he down-shifted at a stop sign, his hand moved off the gearshift lever onto her thigh. Totally distracted by his caressing fingers, she managed to pull her thoughts together long enough to say, "I hope it works. Billy's a sweet bo... Ahh, Tucker, if you're going to do that, you may as well pull over to the curb and—you know."

His laughter swept over her nerve endings like a deep, dangerous current. "Honey, in case you didn't notice, we don't have curbs over here. And as for *you know*, before we can do that again, you're going to have to promise to make an honest man of me come morning."

He pulled over to the ragged edge of the pavement in front of his address, and together they gazed at the tiny bungalow that had been renovated until it resembled an overgrown dollhouse. The lamp in the front window gleamed invitingly, and Hope began to smile. "It's a nice house, Tucker. Cozy. I was always intimidated by that enormous old parsonage over on River Ridge Road—three stories, with ceilings so high you could barely reach the cobwebs on the chandeliers even with a broom! It echoed, did you know that?"

"Darlin', there's one thing you can say for 102 Bias Street—it's not the least bit intimidating." He reached around her to unfasten her seat belt, turning the gesture into a lingering caress, and she pressed herself into his arms with a small sound that drove him half out of his mind. But he was determined not to rush her—not this time.

"Oh, I don't know," she said in a shivery whisper. "I think I'm a little intimidated by that white kitchen floor."

Tucker nuzzled the side of her throat. "Mmmhmm," he murmured against her ear, "Message received—no white kitchen floors. Hell, I'll carpet your kitchen with fur if you think you'd like to walk barefooted on it." *In a nice big house in a nice safe neighborhood....*

"How did we ever get off on kitchen floors?" she whispered. One of these days he was going to have to realize that a dirt-floored soddy would be a palace as long as he was there to share it.

Stirring tendrils of hair against her cheek, he whispered, "Honey, right now if you told me you wanted to set up housekeeping in the middle of the Shacktown Bridge, I'd probably start rolling furniture down the street."

"Starting with the bed, I hope."

He grinned and his late-day beard scraped against her face. "Damn right, starting with the bed. Just give me the luxuries of life and I'll do without the necessities."

After a long, tantalizing kiss that only made matters worse, Hope sat up and fumbled blindly for the door latch. She darted a quick look at Tucker, her dark eyes brimming with love and mischief.

And then she jerked her door open. "Last one in is a rotten egg!"

He caught up with her just before she reached the front porch. Laughing, he swung her around in his arms and then brought her up against him for a noisy, enthusiastic kiss. "Woman, you're asking for it."

"My, aren't we observant tonight," she said with a furious fluttering of long eyelashes.

Somehow, they managed to get inside, and by the time they reached the bedroom door, Hope's shirt was gone, and Tucker had popped the button off the waistband of her shorts. They were both laughing when they fell onto the bed, and he gathered her to him and buried his face in her hair.

"Why do you always smell so good?"

"It must be the sweeping compound I use to keep the dust down," she said modestly.

"I think it has something to do with eating balanced meals and taking vitamins when you were growing up. Nice girls always smell good."

She stroked slowly along his side, from the narrow indentation of his waist upward to the warm hollow under his arm. "Hmmm...how many nice girls have you known well enough to—uh, smell, Tucker?"

"Only one who smelled like nectarines and honeysuckle," he assured her.

Shoving him onto his back, Hope slid up over him. "And we're going to keep it that way, aren't we?"

"Yes, ma'am," he said meekly.

"And we're not going to argue about who lives where and who works where, are we?" And when he didn't answer right away, she took his face between her palms and repeated, "Are we, Tucker?"

"Did I tell you about this theory I have about nice girls growing up to be drill sergeants?"

They tussled on the bed, laughing and rolling over until first Tucker was on top and then Hope was. And then they fell still. Tucker traced the arch of one silken brow with his forefinger, and then he said gravely, "All in the world I want is for you to be happy, Hope. I only want what's best for you—you know that, don't you?"

"Tucker, please—no more tonight, all right?"

"I just pray to God that whatever makes you happy includes me, because I don't think I could stand to lose you now. I don't ever want to hurt like that again."

"Oh, darling," she whispered brokenly, and then she began to make love to him—slowly, her lack of expertise more than made up for by the depth of her feelings.

When Tucker would have switched roles with her, she pushed him gently back down on the bed again. "No—let me. I'm not a girl any longer, Tucker, I'm a woman. And I want to show you—I want to do all the things I've dreamed of doing for so long, and never thought I'd have the chance to do."

Guided only by her own needs and Tucker's reaction, Hope proceeded to live out her fantasies. Kiss by kiss. Touch by touch. Daring caress by daring caress, she explored the powerful body that lay helpless before her.

"Oh, sweet Je-hosephat! Honey, I can't take too much more of this," Tucker groaned when she had nearly driven him out of his mind with her ministrations. "It's my turn now," he said, and grasping her by the shoulders, he dragged her up his body with excruciating slowness.

Hope was in tears by the time they had made love the first time. Tucker merely felt as if he'd been shot out of a rocket launcher. Even before the sweet currents of ecstasy had ebbed completely, the tide of passion began to swell again, and Tucker made slow, delicious love to her, drawing out the pleasure until the last possible moment.

Afterward, they lay barely conscious in the huge bed in the tiny bedroom. Hope had called it wall-to-wall mattress during the hours when she was driving him quietly out of his mind with her sweet loving.

"You cold?" he whispered drowsily.

"Dunno." She slid one of his hands onto her chest. "How do I feel to you?"

"Soft and...better turn on the ceiling fan," he mumbled, but neither of them had the energy to reach for the switch."

It was the sirens that roused Tucker. The sudden tension in his body transmitted itself to Hope, who stirred in his arms. Taking care not to wake her, he slipped out of bed and went to the window. The sky was pitch-dark as far as he could see—evidently the fire was on the other side of town. On the other side of his house, at least.

By the time he had stepped into his jeans and moccasins, Hope was out of bed, fumbling in the near darkness for her own clothes. "What is it?" she asked, worried.

"Dunno yet. Grass fire, probably. Been a lot of those lately."

"Lord, I hate sirens."

"Go back to bed, honey. It's nowhere near here—the fire trucks stopped several blocks away."

But Hope was awake now, and she joined Tucker on the front porch. A few neighbors called a quiet greeting from their own front porches, concern in their sleepy voices as they asked the same questions over and over.

"D'you see where they went?"

"Anybody know what's burning?"

"Don't smell like a brushfire to me."

"Go back to bed, honey—I'm going to drive over and see what's going on," Tucker said, leading Hope back inside. "From the glow, it could be that row of houses over behind the center. Damned Ridgeback landlords—I've told them over and over those places were going to go up like a box of matches one of these nights."

"I'm going with you," Hope announced. While Tucker was digging out a shirt and putting it on, she was hurriedly getting dressed. He didn't argue—she doubted that he'd even heard her, because he went on muttering about lousy wiring and rats and running a pack of no-good money-grubbing politicians out of office and knocking heads together.

It was quite a tirade for a man who had only a short time before shown her a world of passion, tenderness and sensitivity.

"What are you doing? Where do you think you're going?" he demanded suddenly, as if seeing her for the first time.

"The same place you're going."

"The devil you are! If you think I'm letting you go anywhere near that mess, you're crazy, girl!"

"Oh, so now I'm a girl again. Funny—when you want to go to bed with me, I suddenly become a woman, but when you want to throw your weight around and act like the bully you've always been, I turn into a little girl again."

He glared at her for another three seconds before his stern expression gave way to the shamefaced grin. "Okay—woman. You can come with me, but you're staying in the car, you hear? I'm not letting you get out there where you're apt to get run over by a bunch of riffraff or mowed down by a fire hose."

"I'll stand beside the car, but I won't stay inside it."

He expressed himself in a mild oath, and grabbing her hand, sprinted across the porch, the yard, and out to the car.

They both knew before they even got there that the center was on fire. Nothing else on this side of the river stood that tall. Nothing else boasted a square tower with four tall, narrow windows on each side, each window now glowing with an ominous light.

Tucker swore softly, his voice cracking with feeling. "Stay here," he ordered tersely. The door slammed shut behind him and he was gone.

"Owen, over here!" someone shouted, and Tucker skirted a group of onlookers to reach the captain of the fire department.

"Can't you get these people out of here, dammit? Somebody's going to get hurt," Tucker yelled. He surveyed the burning building with a sick feeling. Already the yellow paint looked dark and dingy, even though so far, the fire seemed to be confined to the fourth floor."

"Anything up there?" a fireman asked.

"Damned little. A scaffold, maybe a few cans of paint."

"Paint cloths. Turpentine," another one said with a shake of his head. Two men were holding a three-inch hydrant line, while another was getting ready to break down the main door.

"Dammit, don't bust that door down!" Tucker yelled, running across the wet pavement after him. "I've got a key!"

A ladder truck was maneuvering up close beside the building, and Tucker unlocked the front door and stepped back to watch. It wasn't going to work. The ladder was good for five stories, but these weren't ordinary stories. The ceilings in the first three floors were eighteen feet high.

Another truck arrived at the scene, sirens screaming. Unloading hydrant line as it closed the distance, it dropped off one man at the hydrant and screeched to a stop within a few feet of where Tucker stood.

"There's a hundred pound LP tank outside that house over there," one man yelled. "She's popping off from overpressure. How'd it look when you came by?"

"No flame impingement—yet."

"Get them people the hell outta here!" someone else yelled.

Glass exploded outward from the fourth floor, belching out smoke that glowed ominously pink.

Suddenly, flames appeared in a third floor stairwell window.

"Christ, it's spreading. Get that blasted thing in there, will you? Hooper! Darnell—get a hose on that tank over there, and wet down the first three houses." The orders were being carried out even before the sound of the officer's voice had died away.

People were pressing forward, talking and crying out at each new development. The shorthanded fire department was having trouble containing both the fire and the crowd, so until the police arrived, Tucker took over traffic control duties. He was big enough and furious enough so that no one argued with him when he ordered them back behind the fence.

"You get in the way one more time, I'm gonna come after you, boy, and you're not going to be laughing then," he told one young tough who, on a dare, had climbed up the side of a fire truck.

People were shouting everywhere. The fire itself was unbelievingly noisy. Tucker had just helped an old man wearing striped pajamas and a baseball cap to a pickup truck parked a safe distance away when in a sudden lull, he heard Hope's voice.

"Billy! My God, help him!"

His heart stopped beating, and he dropped the old man unceremoniously onto the tailgate and started back when a woman caught his arm. "Tucker, are we going to lose the day care? Oh, Lordy, my babies was doing so good there, I don't know what I'll—"

"Tucker, Tucker, my boy's done disappeared! You gotta find him for me, Tucker! He promised me he'd stay right here behind the fence, and next thing I knowed, he was—"

"Alma, I'll look for him, but—"

"Oh, please, Lord, I don't know what I'll do if—"

"But you've got to let go my arm," he said through clenched teeth. *Dammit, Hope, I told you to wait in the car!*

"Just find him, that's all I ask," the woman pleaded, and Tucker nodded, his mind on the woman whose cry he had heard coming from the other side of the parking lot. The *wrong* side of the parking lot.

He dodged onlookers, ducked around the tank wagon, his eyes on the glowing, smoke-filled windows of the tower. Grabbing the arm of a booted and black-slickered fireman who was aiming an inch-and-a-half line on the propane tank, he cried, "You seen anything of a woman around here?"

The fireman looked at him like he was crazy, and he knew he deserved it, but he didn't have time to elaborate. "Hope! Dammit, where are you?"

"Woman just ran into the building," the fireman said. "Claimed she saw a kid up there. We tried to stop her, but she slugged Rappoport, messed up his mask, and before he could—"

But Tucker didn't wait to hear the rest. Nausea slammed into him like a hard right cross as he ran toward the open main entrance. *Oh, sweet Jesus, no! Please, God—she wouldn't be that stupid!* He was half praying, half swearing as he dodged fire hoses and ducked past a small cluster of firemen, ignoring their commands that he get the hell out of there before they hauled him out feetfirst.

Later he would remember with shame that he hadn't once thought of Billy. All he could think of was that somewhere in this dark, smoke-filled place, Hope was running out of time, and he had to get to her before she suffocated.

The heat was intense, but the fumes were even worse. Bent double, Tucker ran inside the hallway, calling, coughing, calling again. He couldn't allow himself to think of her being burned, being hurt in any way. It wouldn't happen. He would find her first and get her out of here, and never let her out of his sight again.

At first he thought she must have gone to the day-care area. Only when he found that door still locked did it occur to him that she might have gotten disoriented—it would be easy to do, with smoke rolling down the stairwell, seeping out through the cracks around the elevators, filling the corridors until he had to run crouched over just to see where he was going.

"Hope! Dammit, where are you?" He screamed until he was coughing too hard to scream any more. Fumbling to unlock the doors, he looked into one room after another on the first floor.

Two firemen in full pack trotted up behind him and motioned him to get out. "I can't! She's somewhere inside here! I've got to find her!"

One of the firemen headed for the smoke-filled stairwell, and the other grabbed Tucker by the arm and tried to drag him off by brute force.

"You wanna see daylight again? Let go my arm! Dammit, I know she's in here somewhere—check the other end of the corridor! There's a cleaning closet under the stairwell—check it out and then—"

"Man, I'm telling you, there ain't nobody in here! There was a lady that came in, but she's outta here! She got the boy and we got 'em both out, so come on before—"

Above the horrendous noise, Tucker was aware that someone was talking. The lady—Hope...

"Watch it, he's keelin' over! Austin, grab 'is feet, get the poor sonovabitch outta here and—"

"Tucker! Tucker, oh no..."

"God, here comes that woman again! Hey, lady, you can't come in here! Who the hell's in charge out there?"

Hope was oblivious to the people milling around. The police had arrived, and with them, a sense of order, but all she could see—all she cared about—was Tucker's still form. He was breathing. His heart was beating.

But that was all.

She knelt amidst a forest of legs, but as far as she was concerned, they were alone. Ignoring the noise all around them, she gazed down at the wet, smoke-blackened man lying on the ground, her eyes watering until she could hardly see. A blinding flash of tenderness overcame her, and she realized that she was shaking uncontrollably.

"Hey, ma'am, they think the kid's gonna make it," someone called to her, and she nodded, not really taking in the words.

"Tucker—come on, sweetheart, look at me. You're all right now—you're going to be just fine." He coughed, and she looked up and yelled for a doctor.

Tucker tugged weakly at her arm. "Hope, are you—"

"Doctor! Over here, quickly!" she cried.

"Dammit, I don't need—a doctor," he whispered hoarsely.

"Shh, let me be the judge of that. You need your head examined, for starters."

"I told you to stay by the car," he gasped, and she placed a finger, black with soot, over his lips.

"And I didn't. I know. You can chew me out later on, but right now save your breath, darling."

His red rimmed eyes were startlingly pale against his smoke-darkened skin. Coughing, he tried to sit up, and she pushed him back down again. "Billy?" he gasped.

"Is just fine. I'll tell you all about it later."

"I hate this, dammit." He coughed again, and Hope stroked his face with trembling fingers. She knew how it must gall him to be showing the least weakness.

"Talk to me, girl," he rasped, and she knew she must, or he would keep on questioning her, and he was in no shape for it.

"I saw Billy inside. I tried to tell them, but nobody believed me—they said the building was locked, that nobody could—"

He coughed again, and then swore fiercely, just as another ambulance snarled up to the scene.

"Shh, don't try to talk, love. We can talk later." She stroked his shoulders and smoothed his hair away from his face. He was filthy. He smelled like smoke. His lovely thick hair was in rattails and his skin was the color of putty, and he had never looked more beautiful to her. "Would someone *please* get a doctor over here?" she demanded fiercely. And then, more softly, "You're going to be all right, I promise you, if I have to breathe for you myself. Just lie still and let me look after you."

"Oh, hell, I hate this," he groaned, and she knew he truly did. "I'm the one who should be—"

"Shh, later, love. Here's the EMS crew now." Looking up, she said, "I don't think he's hurt, but he breathed in a lot of smoke. He's coughing, and he feels rather cold to touch, and—"

"If you'd just step aside, ma'am," said one of the team, and Hope moved away, her hand lingering until the last possible moment. She was torn between not wanting to let her beloved out of her sight and wanting the quickest, most thorough medical treatment available for him.

"I'll ride with him," she said when she saw them lifting his limp form onto a stretcher.

"Ma'am, I'm afraid that won't be possible. We're taking the boy in, too, and there's only room for three in the back, counting me."

She nodded. "Yes, of course." Poor Billy—she hadn't even gone over to see how he had fared. As she watched them lift the second stretcher into the back of the orange-and-white wagon, she felt like crying. Instead, she began looking around for someone who could give her a ride to the hospital.

It was nearly noon when Hope led Tucker out to the car and tucked him in as if he were an invalid. He tried to bear it as quietly as possible but his patience was almost at an end. He'd endured all the indignities he could stomach. He had no intention of letting her think he was some kind of a weakling.

"Dammit, it's already seventy-nine degrees in the shade. I don't need a blanket," he grumbled, and Hope laughed.

"You're right, of course. I'm just so glad to get you back—I can't bear it when I think of what might have happened to you."

"I'm okay. But no blankets, and if you start babying me, I'm going to get out and walk home, you got that?"

"You've had a shock, Tucker. It does something to your system."

"You keep on clucking over me like a hen with one chick, I'm going to do something to your system," he grumbled, unwilling to let her know how much he wanted to grab on to her and hold on for dear life. God, he'd never been so scared in all his born days as when he'd thought she was somewhere inside that burning building!

Hope had been examined, as well. A small burn on her left arm had not required dressing and she'd been given a clean bill of health. Gabby had offered to drive them both home, but Hope wouldn't hear of it. Instead, she had collected Tucker's car and hurried back to the hospital.

"What do you suppose is going to happen to Billy?" she asked. She'd looked in on him several times, but as she was not family, the staff would tell her little other than that he would be all right.

"He'll be out of circulation for a while. Smoke inhalation, some second degree burns—nothing too serious, though."

"He looks so miserable. How did he come to be trapped up there?"

Tucker considered his words before he spoke. The fear he had felt when he'd discovered that she was inside the burning building had ebbed, leaving in its wake an uncomfortable mixture of anger and embarrassment. "Best I can figure, he must have been at the center earlier, when we were both there. He probably went in thinking he was going to be alone with you, help you get stuff moved and instead, I showed up. I reckon he got a pretty good eyeful."

"Oh, poor Billy... I never wanted to hurt him."

"Poor Billy, hell! He started the fire that almost—" Tucker broke off. He couldn't allow himself to think of what might have happened when she'd gone chasing in there after that little brat.

"I can't believe Billy meant for things to turn out the way they did, but even if he had set the fire on purpose, why the center? And why the tower? There's nothing up there."

"Why the hell do you think? The center because he considers it ours—I ramrodded the place through, and you work there. Any other questions, Wonder Woman?"

Hope glanced at him warily. "Yes, well . . . uh—why the tower?"

He shrugged. "It's the one floor that isn't sprinklered."

"Tucker, do you think he saw us up there the day of the opening?"

He shrugged again. "Maybe. Who knows? The boy admits he's been starting a few fires lately—since his old man got sent up. Claims he doesn't mean any harm, he just likes to start 'em and then put 'em out."

"You mean like he's controlling them or something," Hope said thoughtfully.

"That's a pretty fair guess. Reckon he figured he's lost control of just about everything else in his life. At least he owned up to it, and he's agreed to talk to one of the doctors there about it."

Hope pulled up in front of Tucker's house and switched off the engine. She felt filthy, although she'd done the best she could with the facilities available to her. Now she didn't know which she wanted most—food, a long, hot shower, or that enormous bed under a lazily turning ceiling fan.

On the other hand, she might have to settle for the guest room. Tucker was in a strange mood. "Tucker, do you want me to help you get settled into bed?"

"Is that an offer?" His eyes glinted like wet flint, cold and hard.

"I only meant—"

"I know what you meant, Hope." He opened his door and got out, leaving her to go or stay as she saw fit.

She hurried after him. "Dammit, it kills you to show any sign of weakness, doesn't it?"

"If you say so." Filthy, smelling of smoke, he had never looked more magnificent. Or more forbidding.

"Tucker!" Halfway up the walk to the house, Hope came to a dead halt. There she waited for him to meet her eyes, and then she said, "We're going to get something settled between us right now, Tucker, or this isn't going to work." She crossed her arms over her chest.

He turned and waited, one brow lifted as if to say, who the hell cares.

She made herself wait until she had reached the porch, took a deep breath and blurted out, "Dammit, you listen to me, Tucker Owen! I don't know what's wrong with you—you're—you're acting childish!"

"Is that so? Okay, now that you've reached that conclusion, may I go inside? Take the car—I'll have someone pick it up tomorrow."

Tears of sheer anger brimming her eyes, Hope charged up the three concrete steps, stopping precisely one foot from where he stood. "I'll tell you what's wrong—you hate being forced to admit that I'm not completely helpless. That I'm a reasonably intelligent, fully capable adult—a fact that you have consistently ignored from the first time I ever saw you!"

"Yeah, right—" A hard smile tugged at the corners of his mouth. "Lemme see, that would be the time you were backed into a corner, while a few gentlemen friends admired your ruffly dress and your hair ribbons, right? If I remember correctly, you handled that in a very adult manner."

Grime was no match for angry hauteur. Her head went back and her brows arched. "Aren't you being a little petty? You know what I mean, and what's more, you're in no shape to stand there arguing. Get in the house and get out of those wet clothes, Tucker."

"Yes*sir*, ma'am!" But he was grinning, his teeth gleaming whitely in a face that still showed more than a trace of smoke damage.

To her dismay, Tucker seemed to have gained the upper hand. Once inside, he turned on all the lights, removed the car keys from her limp fingers and tossed them into the bowl on the living-room table.

Halfway to the kitchen, he asked, "Want some milk?"

Hope nodded, aware of the subtle shift in the balance of power. Never before, and hopefully, never again, would she be in such a perfect position to drive home the fact that she was no fairy-tale princess, but a real live woman, capable of taking care of her man.

"Tucker, aren't you man enough to admit that tonight proved—"

"How about a sandwich? Ham with mustard and horse-radish okay?"

"Fine," she said absently, and got down two glasses for the milk. "Tucker, could we please talk about this?"

"What's to talk about? I'll have a clean-up crew in there as soon as the fire inspectors get done—I doubt there's all that much structural damage, but it'll take a while to—"

"Dammit, would you listen to me?" she shouted.

Startled, Tucker straightened up, a plate of ham in one hand, a jar of horseradish in the other.

"You are doing it to me again," Hope seethed, each word a soft indictment against the man she loved more than anything in this world.

And he was. Shutting her out. Even knowing it, Tucker couldn't stop doing it. When he thought of what she had done today—first for Billy, and then for him—it plain scared the living hell out of him.

He didn't want to think about what had happened. All his life he had tried to protect her—to look after her. And she'd been the one to go into a burning building after him, to see him lying there helpless, coughing his guts out, unable to lift a finger.

"Hope, let me tell you something about the time I went to visit your folks, after I'd heard you'd gone off and gotten married."

She sat down rather suddenly, her face going pale under a surface layer of grime. "I don't see what that has to do with anything."

Tucker continued as if she hadn't spoken. "Your mother was the one who answered the door, but the minute she saw who it was, she called for help. She told me the good news—about how great you were getting along and how happy you were, and then your old man came to the door."

Hope started to interrupt, but Tucker laid a finger across her lips, his eyes never leaving hers. "I didn't get past the front door, you see." His smile held no bitterness, only acceptance. "Maybe I should have gone around to the back, but you know me—pushy as hell. Anyhow, your old man pretty well spelled out things to me. Being a man of the cloth and all that, he had no objections to me as a person. On the other hand, when it came to a son-in-law, that was another matter."

"My boy, I know you mean well, but you must know that Hope has been gently reared. She's not used to your kind of life—it would make her old before her time if she had to go out and grub for a living to make ends meet."

"Of course, I wasn't even through school then—and I had Grandma to take care of. But I had plans. I would have been able to take care of you."

"You'll never be able to give her what she needs—a delicate, fragile girl like our Hope. She deserves a husband who can take good care of her, and I'm happy to say she now has one."

"I told him we loved each other. I told him we'd made plans for the future, but it didn't cut much ice. By then, it was already too late."

"Being the sweet girl she is, my boy, I'm sure Hope would try to fit into your—uh, surroundings. She'd never complain, not our Hope, but you and I know she deserves more than you can ever give her. And young man, I'm happy to be able to tell you that this discussion is academic, because Hope was married not two weeks ago. I myself performed the ceremony, and a lovelier bride I have never had the pleasure of seeing."

Hope stared at her entwined fingers. What could she say—that she was surprised? She wasn't. That her father had lied? He hadn't—at least not according to his view. He honestly thought he had done what was best for her.

Dear Lord, so this was what Tucker had been fighting all these years—her father had made him believe he wasn't good enough for her, that he wasn't capable of taking care of her. No wonder he had worked so hard to prove otherwise!

"I can never tell them, Tucker," she said softly.

Pain etched itself across his features, and he nodded. Seeing it, she reached out and covered his hand with hers. "Oh, no—not what you're thinking! Not about us. I only meant I can never let them know how wrong they were. How close they came to ruining my life. It would kill them, don't you see? They only did what they thought was right for me."

Tucker reserved judgment. For her sake, he would try and forget the past. He was going to have all he could handle just to deal with the present. "Yeah, honey, I know. Maybe I can win some points by letting your old man know that I'm not only willing, but I'm now perfectly capable of taking over the job of looking after you."

Her hand slid away from his and she leaned back in her chair, surveying him coolly. "Oh? And *who* pulled *whom* out of a burning building a few hours ago?"

"Dammit, are you going to keep bringing that up for the next hundred years?"

"If I need to."

Tucker unwrapped the platter of ham and began hacking off slices. "Then might I remind you that I wouldn't have been in the damned building in the first place if you hadn't gone charging in where you had no business being?"

"That's beside the point and you know it. Tucker, answer one question—do you honestly think I'm incapable of making a serious decision that will affect the rest of my life?"

Warily, he thought over possible pitfalls and then said, "About burning buildings?"

"Don't be ridiculous."

"Oh. You mean about marrying me. Well, uh...sure you're capable, honey. Otherwise, I'd have applied for adoption papers."

"Fine, then I'm equally capable of deciding where I want to spend the rest of my life, right?"

"Whoa, now—"

"Whoa, nothing. You answered your own question. Now, unless you're the worst possible case of male chauvinism, you'll agree that I have as much right to decide where we live as you do."

"Ah...I don't know about this chauvinism business, honey, but there are some things a man—"

"So you must know that the only practical thing to do is stay right here at 102 Bias Street, because it's close to your work and mine, and if I decide to start teaching a class in—"

Tucker frowned. "Hold on there—last I heard, you were going to take a class, not teach one."

"—in remedial reading at the center, then that'll be convenient, too. I know a retired English teacher who just might be interested in setting it up."

"Got it all figured out, haven't you?" He placed a thick, untidy sandwich on a paper towel in front of her, and poured two glasses of milk.

"Yes, I believe so. Did I leave out anything?"

Tucker sat down across the table from her, his long legs deliberately embracing hers under the table. "Just a few incidentals, but I can fill 'em in for you. Number one, we're getting married just as soon as we can cut through all the red tape."

Laying aside his sandwich in an impatient gesture, he came around to her side of the table and covered her shoulders with a hard, warm grip. "Number two, I'm getting Miss Eula to fill in for you for the next two weeks."

"Oh, but—"

"Don't worry, Gabby'll keep her in line. A little discipline never hurt a kid anyway, and Miss Eula's mellowed a lot these past few years."

"Now wait a minute, I'm not sure—Two weeks?"

Hope was weakening. Good. Because his strength was returning rapidly, and with it, the desire he always felt whenever she was near. Kneeling, he removed her damp sandals and began massaging the soles of her feet. She'd always had sensitive arches, and he was counting on it now.

When her head lolled back, he breathed a sigh of relief. "Then, there's our honeymoon...." he went on.

"Don't tell me," she said drowsily, "we're going to Daytona. Or Talladega."

He stroked her calves and gradually moved higher. "Ah, come on now, you don't think I'm going to share you with a few hundred thousand race fans, do you? No way. I've got a cabin way up in the Smokies where the nights are so cold we'll need a foot of blankets to keep warm." Tucker's eyes gleamed softly in anticipation.

"Oh, do you think so?" Twisting around in her chair, Hope ran her fingertips over the ridge of his brow, drawing them down over his temples to cradle his face between her hands. And then she smiled, melting him completely.

"Woman, when you look at me like that, you can ask for anything in the world and it's yours."

"Does that include a bath? I'm tired of smelling like smoke." Hope laughed, and for reasons he didn't even try to understand, Tucker laughed, too. "What are you thinking?" she murmured.

He brushed her hair back from her face and kissed both her eyelids. Then he lifted her up in his arms, and for a wonder, she didn't object, not even a little squawk. "Oh, I dunno...a lot of things. Like, is my shower going to be big enough for both of us, because I really need to get clean, but I don't think either one of us ought to be by ourselves. And whether I should take time to put away the food, because it might be a while before we get back to it. But most of all, I guess what I was really thinking was that once in a blue moon, a guy gets this lucky. I thought I'd lost you."

"Not in a million years, love."

"Your hair's still wet. My shampoo doesn't smell like honeysuckle, but you're welcome to use it."

He had her shirt unbuttoned by the time they reached the bathroom, and then he started in on her shorts.

"I'll throw these things in the washer as soon as we get through in here," he said, and she only smiled.

Tucker shed the rest of his clothes while Hope adjusted the water temperature, and then she turned around. "Honestly, Tucker, you don't have to get in here with me, I'll be just fine."

"Just pretend I'm not here. It's strictly a safety measure, in case either one of us starts feeling faint or anything. Don't worry, I'll be quiet—you won't even know I'm around."

Lathering both her hands, Hope placed them on Tucker's shoulders and let them trail down his big wet body. "If the day ever comes when I don't know you're around, then I'll definitely be in need of a keeper," she whispered.

"You got it, sweetheart. Lifetime contract, all guarantees and options."

And he started demonstrating a few of the options.

* * * * *

Diamond Jubilee Collection

It's our 10th Anniversary...
and *you* get a present!

This collection of early Silhouette
Romances features novels written
by three of your favorite authors:

ANN MAJOR— *Wild Lady*
ANNETTE BROADRICK— *Circumstantial Evidence*
DIXIE BROWNING— *Island on the Hill*

* These Silhouette Romance titles were first published in the early 1980s
and have not been available since!

* Beautiful Collector's Edition bound in antique green simulated leather to
last a lifetime!

* Embossed in gold on the cover and spine!

This special collection will not be sold in retail stores and is only available
through this exclusive offer.

Look for details in all Silhouette series published in June, July and August.

COMING SOON...

For years Harlequin and Silhouette novels have been taking readers places—but only in their imaginations.

This fall look for PASSPORT TO ROMANCE, a promotion that could take you around the corner or around the world!

Watch for it in September!

★